The Leftover Kid

ESPECIALLY FOR GIRLS™ presents

The Leftover Kid

Carol Snyder

Pacer Books

a member of The Putnam Publishing Group

New York

Edited for Weekly Reader Books and published
by arrangement with Pacer Books.

Printed in the United States of America

Library of Congress Cataloging-in-Publication Data

Snyder, Carol.   The leftover kid.
Summary: While doing a life cycle project at school,
eighth-grader Wendy experiences first hand some of
the good and bad aspects of family life when her
older brother, his wife, and baby and her grandparents move in with Wendy and her parents.
   [1. Family life—Fiction] I. Title.
PZ7.S68517Le 1986   [Fic.]   85-29878
ISBN 0-448-47773-4

Dedicated to the continued

strength of today's families

and to the memory of my mother

SHIRLEY GLASBERG

a woman ahead of her time

wife, mother,

grandmother, businesswoman

and treasured friend

The Leftover Kid

1.

I THOUGHT THE day would never end. Everyone seemed in high gear in school this afternoon, as if stress was their middle name. That's how my mother would have described it. During last period, my French teacher, Mrs. Smith (isn't that a ridiculous name for a French teacher?) got hyper just because when she said, "No one is to get out of their seat," I moved, seat and all. I slid my chair from one side of the room to the wastepaper basket in the front to throw out a tissue. Of course the class cracked up laughing as I moved my chair back to my desk.

My French teacher has no sense of humor though. All she seems to say, or all I've learned from her, are the words, *"Silence! Silence! S'il vous plaît."* Quiet, quiet if you please. And *"Crachez votre chewing-gum."* Spit out your chewing-gum. Today she spoke to me in English. Loud and clear. "Wendy Meyer, you have detention," she said.

"I'll have to check my calendar. I'll see when I can schedule you," I answered. "Tomorrow is taken already with detention from Mr. Murdock." I wasn't even saying this to be funny or fresh. It was true. But the kids around me laughed some more. Mr. Murdock's the music teacher who didn't go for my method of musical book covers—using one book cover for all my books, just switching it to the next book each period like musical chairs. With this school's rules you'd think an uncovered book was a federal offense. What really got me mad was that Sherman Barker, the kid who'd announced that my other books were uncovered, didn't even have his book with him at all! Because of him my parents will have to sign a detention slip and I'll have to listen to a lecture.

My French teacher, Mrs. Smith, said, *"Je ne sais pas. Votre soeur Kerry, quelle bonne fille."*

"I don't know," I translated her words in a whisper to my friend Jennifer, who sits next to me. "Your sister Kerry, what a good girl. But my sister Kerry is not me," I added. "The only way we're alike is that we both have curly dark hair and we can talk to each other about anything." I turned Mrs. Smith's words into a joke, but deep down I wanted to shout—*I am me!*

By now I was anxious to get home to my peaceful, quiet house where I could sip cold milk to wash down Oreo cookies, watch *General Hospital,* and not have a care in the world.

I walked home with Jennifer. She was upset about being paired with Sherman Barker for the coed health project that began today. Our other friend Brenda didn't walk with us this afternoon. She had basketball practice to go to, and gorgeous Robby Marshall, who she'd been paired with, walked her to the gym to discuss the three-week health project: "The Life Cycle— Babies to Old Age." Week one we'll be studying infancy and childhood; week two, teenage and adult mid-life years, and week three will be about old age. Mrs. Devin had explained it was to help us better understand ourselves and our families.

I wished once again that I'd been paired with Robby. But instead I'd been paired with Gary Weiss, who for years has held the title "class clown," and who now was nowhere in sight. Since kindergarten he's walked to and from school with me and my friends but lately, on some days, he races home ahead of all of us. I don't know why. He doesn't invite us home anymore, either. Some big help Gary was going to be. I remember when he helped me get an F in fourth grade instead of my usual A. We'd been paired to work on this social studies unit about the Louisiana Territory. One of the questions we had to answer was, "Why were Lewis and Clark selected to lead the exploration of the Louisiana Territory and blaze a new trail to the Pacific Ocean?"

We wrote, "Because they knew how to get there." When the teacher marked us wrong, Gary complained by asking her a question. "Lewis and Clark were chosen to lead an exploration of the Louisiana Territory because they didn't know how to get there?" A lot of kids laughed. The teacher did not. She gave us and our project an F for "failure to take it seriously."

Now with Gary as my partner in this project, we even sound like a comedy team, Meyer and Weiss. True, with Gary I might have some funny moments, but with Robby Marshall there'd be romance. I wondered if Gary'd really come over at three o'clock as he'd said. And if he did, should I let him in without my parents' permission. They both work. I'm a latchkey kid. Gary's last words to me this afternoon, just before he raced off, were, "Have the cookies waiting, sweetheart," but with this routine he has a few things to learn about women's liberation.

The colorful autumn leaves from the elm and maple trees of my Brooklyn neighborhood crunched under our feet, and I thought about the big piles of them at the curb and how great it was when Jennifer and I were younger and used to jump in them and bury each other. My mother used to yell that she could smell me coming home from a block away. I wonder if growing up and becoming independent means I better stop thinking about the way things used to be.

When I got to my house, I fumbled around my neck for the shoelace tucked inside my sweatshirt. Then, following my mother's instructions, I checked to make sure the door wasn't "ajar" as she calls it. If the door *was* "ajar," she said I shouldn't go in, but should go to a neighbor's. I laughed when she told me that, because how can a door be a jar? It's a door. Why can't she just say "open," like other people?

I rang the doorbell to let any possible burglars know that I was home, then put my books down on the mat outside the front door. The telephone was ringing and I struggled with the double lock, hurrying to get in before the ringing stopped. I don't do well under pressure and, sure enough, by the time I got to the phone in the front hall just inside, the last ring had rung and all I heard when I lifted up the receiver was a dial tone.

My imagination immediately took over. Maybe it was someone terrific like Robby, home already and asking a question about the life cycle project. I might have come to his rescue and he would see that he really likes me a lot. Or maybe it was my grandmother Minnie, calling from Florida to invite me for a visit. But all the time I knew it was my mother, calling from work as usual, to see if I got home safe and sound. She'd call back later, next chance she was free. She's a court stenographer and is very busy. She says she got a job to help pay my brothers' and sister's college expenses. She's been working for six months now. But I think she'd work even if we were millionaires, because she loves it.

Once I got my books from the mat outside, I closed and double-bolted the door, then stopped to identify all house noises before going any farther. It was quiet except for the click of the furnace and the leaky faucet dripping in the kitchen. Occasionally I heard a squeak of unknown origin, but when I listened again it was a familiar squeak, not to be worried about. I never used to think about these things, even when Kerry was in high school and stayed late for drama club. I knew she'd be home soon, so coming home first was no big deal.

I picked up the mail from the tile floor under the mail slot in the door and scanned through the envelopes. "Bills, bills, bills," I mimicked my father. I talk to myself out loud a lot so my vocal cords won't dry up.

"Darn!" I said. "No mail for me."

I walked through the dining room into the kitchen, dumping my books and purse on the kitchen table and grabbing the note Mom had left for me.

13.

Wendy baby,

I have to be at night court in Manhattan. Daddy is meeting me there after his sales conference and we're eating out. I can't phone you this afternoon. I have a frantic schedule so just call my office and tell the secretary you're home safe.

Now I really wondered who'd phoned before. I also thought about the leftovers they'd bring me from the restaurant. I hoped for a lobster claw although I'd probably get an eggroll. They don't eat dinner out too often, but when they do they always bring me something. I think they feel guilty for not taking me with them. I read on.

There's leftover roast chicken and potatoes in the refrigerator. Also, please fold the laundry and empty the dishwasher. I'll phone you tonight. I've got big news for you! Can't wait to hear your reaction.
Have a good day and be sure to lock the door. Don't open it if you're not expecting a friend.
Love,
Mom

No. I'm going to open it to seedy-looking strangers, enemies, and perverts. When have I ever forgotten to lock the door? And what is with this mysterious news bit? I think my parents make up for not being home by worrying while they're away. They make such a big deal about my being home alone.

What my parents don't realize is that I love being home alone. When my brothers Steve and Alan left for college, my sister Kerry was still around, but when she first left for college two months ago, I was bored stiff. I used to look forward to talking to her when she'd get home from school. But then I realized I can talk to her on the phone. She calls every week. Now when my friends call or I call them, there's nobody to tell me to get off the phone. I can talk as long as I want. When Mom and Dad come home, I get all the attention at dinner. I can tell about my entire day without a single interruption. There's also no fighting about who's taking a shower when and for how long. There's no one to tell on me when I do something wrong. And three words I never hear anymore or say anymore are, "She started it!"

I'm giving myself independence lessons—lessons in growing up and not needing my family so much. After all, in only five years I'll be going off to college. I want to be ready to exist on my own. I once read in *Teen* magazine that you should set your goals five years ahead so you know who you are and where you're going. I'm giving myself these independence lessons so I can become me—whoever that is. I've always been somebody's kid or sister till now and, most annoying of all, the baby of the family. My mother still calls me Wendy baby. But Kerry named me the leftover kid because I wear her leftover clothes, ride a leftover bike, my favorite food is Thanksgiving dinner leftovers, and now I get left home by my family. But I like it.

Yeah, it's good to be a leftover kid. My life is just perfect as is.

After I called and checked in with Mom's secretary, I took a box of Oreo cookies and a glass of milk, carefully carrying them to the coffee table in the living room. I turned on the TV and curled up in my favorite spot, on the velvety blue carpeting in the corner.

General Hospital had just started and Luke was ranting about something or other. I carefully separated the two chocolate cookies and had a mouthful of luscious cream filling. I ate as many Oreos as I wanted and watched TV till I had to answer the phone.

"Hey, little mama, it's your one and only here." Gary's voice has a laugh built into it.

The "little mama" refers to the fact that for the first week of this life cycle project, the part about infants and childhood, we are supposed to pretend to be married and parents of an infant. Our teacher, Mrs. Devin, divided the class into coed couples and handed each a photo of a real baby from the infant care center for working parents. There were equal numbers of boys and girls in the class, but there was one set of twin infants, a male and a female. Gary and I volunteered to take the twins.

It didn't seem right to me to separate twins. One would have been a leftover. How much more work could one extra baby be? Anyway, I relate to leftovers, especially leftover babies with the biggest, darkest eyes you ever saw and heads full of dark hair. I love babies even more since my oldest brother Steve's baby was born three weeks ago. It's very exciting to become an aunt. I've seen my nephew Jory two times, but my sister-in-law Marissa won't let me hold him. "He hasn't had his shots yet," she'd said. "I never heard of anyone getting rabies from a baby," I'd told her. Not only did she not laugh, she didn't even smile. My parents kiss Jory from his head to his toes. It's not fair.

Mrs. Devin is the first to teach this course at eighth grade level. She feels high school, where this project is usually done, is not soon enough. She told us she was glad to be permitted even three weeks to teach this course, although that's not much time. "It will be a telescoped view of life," she'd said. "But life does sometimes move fast, and changes can take place one day to the next."

"Gary," I couldn't help chuckling a little into the phone receiver. "I'm glad you finally called since you were supposed to be here by now."

"My mom's not home from work at the bank yet," he said, and I thought he was being serious until he added, "I guess you might say she's been held up at the bank! She's usually home by three-fifteen at the latest. I call her my American Express card. I can't leave home without her . . . never mind why. So I won't be coming over to your house today."

When he said that last sentence, he suddenly sounded very serious and kind of sad, but then he covered up with a joke.

"Anyway, Mrs. Devin said we can give our babies nicknames to make them our own," Gary said. "I think we should call the boy Askhim, so when the teacher says, 'What's his name?' we can tell her, 'Askhim,' and you know Mrs. Devin, she'll talk to the photo and say, 'What's your name?' and we can say again, 'Askhim.' I figure we can take up a good ten minutes of class time with that one."

17.

That sounded like fun to me. "Sure," I said. "Why not?" Gary was like an Olympic champion of wasting class time. Even way back in third grade when we were studying Indians, he once hung himself up on a hook in the wardrobe with a bathing cap over his blond wavy hair so he'd look scalped. He was tall for his age even then, so it was easy for him to hang his jacket on a hook and get into it. He has perfect timing for things like that, and at exactly the right moment he maneuvered open the sliding doors with his foot and screeched. I can still remember that he wasted a good fifteen minutes of class time. The teacher scolded him. She said, "Indians did many valuable and important things. We are learning history here, not playing cowboys and Indians."

"And I think we should name the girl Spot," I continued.

"Spot?" Gary said. "What kind of name is that for a baby?"

"I've always wanted to have a dog named Spot. For over a year now I've been begging my parents to let me get a dog. Any kind would be okay with me. Have you seen those adopt-a-dog ASPCA commercials on TV?" I asked.

"Sure," Gary said. "They're on a lot."

"Well, I'd love to adopt one of those dogs. I asked my parents but they have about a million reasons why their answer is no."

"Like what?" Gary really sounded interested, and I went on even though I didn't mean to.

"Two weeks ago when I asked about this cute little white poodle, my father said, 'The only dog for us right now is a hot dog. Come on Wendy. Let's go to Nathan's Famous Hog Dogs at Coney Island.' Last Sunday when I asked about a tiny miniature Doberman pinscher, they had a long reason about not wanting to be tied down now with responsibilities. I could tell a dog anything," I went on. "It would be there to listen and it wouldn't talk back."

"I know what you mean," Gary said. "I don't have a dog either. So agreed," he added. "The babies' names are Askhim and Spot. And I'll do that crib design Mrs. Devin asked for. I like to do things like that. See ya tomorrow." We hung up.

I really enjoyed having the house to myself. First, I did my homework with the TV blaring. Then, while my stereo blasted out rock music, I worked on making these picture frames out of scraps of pretty colored wool and cardboard from my dad's shirts. I bring the frames to the nursing home on Coney Island Avenue, where I do volunteer work. The elderly sick people there are so nice. They love to get presents, and they're always there if I don't feel like being alone at my house. I like cheering people up. I don't tell people I do this. I don't usually let my feelings show. I just prefer joking and being a comedienne in school.

Next I folded the laundry and emptied the dishwasher, making up fake news announcements like, "Dish runs away with spoon—more at eleven." Then I took out my collection of travel brochures and spread them all out on the floor of my room. I've collected them for three years now. I have a subscription to *Holiday* magazine and clip the "send for this brochure free of charge." I really send for them. They're beautiful. I have this real cool glossy brochure with pictures of sparkling blue waters and wonderful words describing Nova Scotia. It's my favorite. What I love about this hobby is that at least once a week I get mail. I love to get mail.

I took out the leftover roast chicken from the refrigerator. Since I have been eating chicken for days already I checked under my arms for feathers. Mom mass-produced cooked chickens a few nights ago so she wouldn't be bothered with meals this week.

I ate my dinner in the dining room on the good dishes, pretending I was in Nova Scotia at a fancy hotel eating pheasant under glass like in my brochures. I put the photos of the babies at places I'd set for them at the table. I found myself saying things like, "Stop spitting, it's good to try new foods," and "Oh sweet babies, eat up all your din-din." Okay, so it sounds more like I was feeding Morris the Cat on TV, but I meant it lovingly.

After I cleaned up I took a bubble bath and tried on my mother's bra to see how much more I have to grow. It's much more. I think my sister filled out much faster than me. She also grew taller than I'll ever grow. Next I put on my pajamas with the soft lace around the neck, the kind that doesn't scratch or tickle. I don't take dance lessons but I danced in front of the mirror as I sang the score of *A Chorus Line*. I saw the show on Broadway for my birthday and I bought the tape. I was up to "Gimme the ball, gimme the ball, gimme the ball," when the phone rang. Everything had been perfect till my mother on the other end couldn't resist telling me what she thought was great news.

"I'm so glad you're okay," she greeted me. "Sorry I couldn't get to call. I can't wait another minute to tell you the big news. Are you ready for this, Wendy? It's the best news for all of us."

"What's the news?"

"Here goes," she said. "Your brother Steve and Marissa and the baby are going to live with us for a while till Steve finishes medical school. Isn't that great? You won't have to be alone so much. Daddy and I won't have to worry, and Steve, Marissa, and Jory can get out of the university housing and save money. It's a perfect arrangement! I'll have my first and only, best-in-the-whole-world baby grandson in kissing distance. And Marissa is such a helpful, take-charge person. Thank goodness she's not the kind of daughter-in-law you have to wait on hand and foot."

For a minute I was speechless. "I know you're overcome with joy," said my mother, the optimist. "I thought I'd have more time to prepare you but this has turned into an emergency housing solution. Daddy and I will be home late so we'll talk more tomorrow. I've got to go now. This is a pay phone and I'm out of change."

"Ma," was all I could get out before she hung up.

I was overcome all right. But it wasn't joy I was feeling. Won't be alone so much? Won't be alone at all was more like it. I love my nephew but I just don't want him on my turf. I bet my parents won't even notice me with Jory here. How could I dance around and sing out loud with a houseful of people. I'd feel like a jerk. And Marissa here twenty-four hours a day to boss me around and tell me not to breathe on the

21.

baby. What about my independence? This was a low blow all right. I hung up and walked through each room of my beautiful empty house savoring the silence and feeling this creepy nervousness like pending doom, just as on *General Hospital* before a crisis moment.

2.

MOM DIDN'T GO to work the next day because she'd worked at court last night and because she wanted to help Marissa, Steve, and Jory move in. She made not quite cooked scrambled eggs and toasted English muffins for Dad and me to eat for breakfast.

"I can't eat these eggs," I said. "They're still moving."

"Wendy, watch your mouth," Dad said.

"Since when don't you like scrambled eggs?" Mom said, tightening the doubled belt she'd borrowed from me to wear with her blue sweater dress. I used to borrow her stuff a lot. Now since she works she's always borrowing my earrings, belts, or bracelets—to "pull together an outfit," she calls it. She's small for her age, forty-seven, and I'm about average for my age, thirteen. We look a little alike except she's rounded and I'm almost flat. She's got dark brown, straight hair with glimmers of red in it if she's in the sun. My hair is dark and curly. I think she's pretty. So does my father.

He wolf-whistles at her every morning.

"Your mother cooked you a nice breakfast," Dad said. "Just eat and say thank you or get up and cook the eggs some more yourself. You didn't even complain the other day when I made three-minute eggs in one-and-a-half minutes," he added, and brushed a crumb that got stuck in his newly grown mustache. I can't get used to it. I end up staring at the mustache and don't hear what he says.

"When it's my turn to cook breakfast we'll have cold cereal and fruit," I said. "That starts out well-done."

I cooked the eggs some more, and as we ate I told my parents about the baby photos I have to carry around and about the infant care center for working parents. "I'm paired with Gary Weiss," I said. "And we have to read about baby care and keep a baby log and then we'll have two other week-long projects on mid-life and old age. We're supposed to learn to understand ourselves and other people better."

"I love when you're encouraged to use your imagination," Mom said, and I gave her my "I'm not a baby" look. "And what a good idea to study the different stages of life. When do you get to middle age?" She seemed quite interested. "I could use some understanding," she added. I explained this was only the second of five days of infancy and childhood. As I'd hoped, my parents were reminded of another infant, Jory.

"Well, we'll certainly have a twenty-four-hour-a-day study of infancy in this house," Dad added, then laughed as if it was a joke. But I wasn't exactly sure how funny he thought it was. My Dad's been grumpy lately, and this overly cheerful voice sounded just a bit phony to me.

"I've got so much to do this morning to get ready for the kids to move in," Mom said. "I can't wait to kiss that baby. I want to decorate a perfect room for my perfect grandson. I'm going to put the baby in Alan's room and Marissa and Steve can have Kerry's room since it used to be Steve's room in the first place."

Alan is my other brother. He's a junior at the University of Hartford. No one knows what he's studying.

"Aren't you excited, Wendy?" Mom said. "You won't be alone after school anymore. I didn't want to discuss the move with you until it was definite. Only it went from the talk stage to emergency stage when the boiler broke down and there was no hot water in the old university housing. Marissa was frantic."

"Well, one good thing is that this house will be alive again," Dad said, as if convincing himself.

"What is it—dead—with only me?" I asked, letting my opinion of this whole situation be known in the tone of my voice.

"Of course it's not dead with only you. We've loved having you all to ourselves," Dad said.

"Then why are we taking in stray families?"

"They're our family and they need us," Mom said in a tone that implied "and that's that." "They need the financial help and something is always breaking down in that old apartment."

"So how come you wouldn't take in one stray dog who needed us too?" I reminded them of the adopt-a-dog commercial on TV Sunday and the miniature pinscher that I'd begged to adopt and name Spot. "Your reason for saying no that day was, and I quote,

'We don't want to be tied down with an animal at this time of our life when the kids are going off and we have more freedom.'"

"You're comparing a stray dog to your very own baby nephew?" Dad said. "Give it a chance, Wendy. We're talking about the best and most gorgeous baby in the world coming to live with us. I have to admit that much."

"You both leave and go to work. Your lives will hardly change. I'll have to help with the baby—but from a distance because Marissa doesn't like me to get too close. And I'll be here with Marissa bossing me around. You know how she is. Don't I even get asked for an opinion before you change my life?" I didn't wait for an answer. I grabbed my baby photos, placed them into paper cups for cribs and stuffed them into my pocketbook. I gathered my books, not caring that papers flew out of my loose-leaf, and without even saying good-bye I stormed out.

Mom called after me, "Wendy honey—what could we do? Please try to understand."

I jogged to the corner of Tenth and Avenue K, mumbling, "Try to understand . . . try to understand." I arrived even before Jennifer and Brenda. I wondered if the siren I heard sing by on Ocean Parkway was a police car or an ambulance and where it was going and why. I do that a lot because you hear a lot of sirens in Brooklyn. It took my mind off my own worries.

I put my books down on the sidewalk and twirled myself around the lamppost on Avenue K. My imagination was working overtime picturing a house on fire, a dog licking its owner to wake it up, and a fireman coming just in time. I always imagine happy endings. I didn't even notice when Robby Marshall approached. I wish I had.

"Don't you get dizzy doing that?" he asked.

"Just a little," I said, staggering away from the pole and blushing with embarrassment.

"You know I'm really getting into this baby photo stuff. Want to see what I made?" he asked.

"Sure," I said, getting closer to him. Close enough to smell the talcum powder on the back of his neck. He'd built a crib for his baby photo out of balsa wood. It looked real, with bumpers made out of shelving-paper trim and bars on tiny paper-clip hinges that you could put up or down.

"That is so neat," I said.

"Want me to make one for you?" he asked.

"Would you? That would be great. Only I need two. Remember?" I pointed to my pocketbook like a jerk and said, "Twins."

"Oh yeah, I forgot. I'll make two then." Maybe he does like me, I figured, until he added, "They only cost a dollar each."

What, was I gonna look like a cheapo and say no, never mind? I simply left my order for two baby cribs and figured I'd split the cost with Gary, who was only drawing crib designs. Robby is such a businessman. Even in first grade he painted rocks and sold them for a penny each as paperweights.

Jennifer and Brenda arrived.

Jennifer apparently is ignoring this whole baby business, making believe it's not even happening. I guess that's her way of dealing with Sherman Barker as father. I really feel badly for her. She said he's such a jerk. He copied so much on the Iowa tests that he copied someone else's birth date.

Brenda took the baby photo in its crib from Robby. "You're terrific," she said to him. He smiled his dimpled smile at her and their fingers touched since he hadn't let go of the cribs yet. I wished I was Brenda. She's an only child, has the prettiest face, and a huge closet with sliding doors. Inside it she has sweaters in every color—even colors I didn't know the name of till she told me—like puce and mauve. And now she even had Robby Marshall as her partner. How lucky could you get?

Gary, on the other hand, arrived and slapped me on the back. "Where are the babies?" he asked as if he were accusing me of foul play.

"In my pocketbook over there." I pointed. "Gary!" I yelled. "Stop it!" But it was too late.

He went right over to my pocketbook, put his hands inside, and pulled out the two paper cup cribs, dumping out my wallet, my lip gloss, eye shadow, old ticket stubs from the Midwood movie theater, and my mirror that lights up.

After Gary did a balancing act with the paper cups in the palms of his hands singing, "Da da da dah, da dah da da dah," he threatened to juggle the babies next. I got them back and we headed for school.

During my morning classes I found myself fiddling around in my pocketbook now and then to check on my babies. I also kept thinking about Jory, Marissa, and Steve crowding me out of my house. Well, soon Gary and I would introduce our babies, Askhim and

Spot, to the class. That would take my mind off my problem. I guess I was smiling at the thought. "Wipe that smile off your face, Meyer, and get to work," Mr. Barston, my science teacher said.

In fourth period, health, everyone was showing off their handiwork of crib designs, part of last night's homework assignment to make us aware of the importance of safety features for baby furniture. Like crib bars shouldn't be too far apart because a baby could get its head caught. We'd discussed this in class, yesterday.

"My baby was bad last night," Gary complained.

"Big shot," I said. "You didn't even have the babies with you last night."

"Hey, Jennifer," Gary said, "where's your baby photo?"

"Ask Sherman," she muttered. "He insisted on taking it home with him yesterday, only he dropped it and it went down a sewer. You know what the jerk tells me this morning?"

"What?" I asked. "No wonder you look so upset. That's awful." At least she was talking about it now. That also explained why she seemed to be ignoring the project. I felt so sad for her. She looked so disappointed.

"He tells me he gave our baby photo—our already named Susan Beth—a burial at sea. Can you believe this kid? And, my luck, I have to be paired with him."

"Sorry, Jen," I said soothingly, and put my arm around her shoulder to comfort her. I clutched my pocketbook and thought of my baby photos, glad they were safe and well. But I felt guilty for thinking this when Jennifer was so sad.

Mrs. Devin got our attention. As she handed out assignment sheets, she asked us to tell our babies' names. The good old "Askhim" name got a huge laugh from the class, so did Spot. Gary and I shook hands on a job well done. Mrs. Devin said she enjoys a joke as much as the next person, but she asked us to promise that we would take the project seriously. We said we would and she let us keep the names.

The assignment sheet instructed:

Baby log

> Your baby log should include information on the baby's physical and mental development and begin with Entry #1, early infancy. Since we have limited time, we will imagine that each day of the photo baby's life is equivalent to six months of a real baby's. You are to research infant and child behavior and development information from your textbook, *Child Care and Development* by Louise Bates Ames, and apply it to the way you take care of your photo baby. Also to be included in your log is a daily record of your comments, reactions, and problems relating to the care of your baby.

I bet my sister-in-law, Marissa, knows everything there is to know about babies and will tell me so when she moves in. She's really smart, besides being a know-it-all. Actually she's perfect. She researches everything. She read back issues of *Consumer Reports* before she bought a corn popper. I bet she even does research on the best toilet paper to buy. She keeps coupons in a file folder where she can find them in her pocketbook. She even has them with her in the supermarket when she needs them, not like my mom, dad, or me. I bet she's going to organize us and change everything. I bet I'm going to hate this entire arrangement.

"Why so glum, dear?" Gary said to me. I hadn't realized my feelings were showing. I don't usually let that happen. It kind of surprised me that Gary would even notice. He'd never noticed my feelings before, and we've been friends for years.

"Someday when you have a lot of hours to spare I'll tell you," I said. Then I switched back quickly to my usual joking self. "In the meantime, buster—ya better help with these here young-uns or my pappy will be after you with some buckshot."

"Yes, ma'am," he joked back. "I'll take the babies tonight. Askhim and Spot come to Dada."

I handed over the two paper cups. "Can you handle this?" I asked.

Gary answered, "Can I handle this, she asks. Piece of cake."

I, on the other hand, was not so sure.

3

I COULD FEEL the difference in the house from the moment I walked in. It started with the overpowering smell of baby powder and Baby Magic lotion. The entire house smelled like freshly bathed baby.

Okay, so it's a delicious smell. But I'd rather the house smell of pizza, popcorn, or better yet, wet dog fur.

Then I heard that "wah uh wah uh wah" of new-baby crying. It seemed quite clear that my opinion not only wasn't asked for around here, but didn't even matter when I gave it. That really bugged me. I'd hoped maybe Mom and Dad would reconsider and change the plans. But Steve, Marissa, and Jory had already moved in against my wishes and they sure hadn't wasted a moment. I thought I'd have at least till after *General Hospital*. I didn't think they'd do it this fast. But then again, when Marissa decides to do something, it's immediately if not sooner.

The first thing I thought of as I closed the door behind me was, Why is that baby crying like that? What is Marissa doing to him? And my second thought was, How can life change so from one day to the next? I walked into the kitchen and dumped my books on the table. I didn't expect to see the refrigerator door open and a pair of ankles and high heels under it. Marissa is tall and blond and could have been a model but she was more interested in computers. She still dresses in skirts and high heels as if she's going to work in an office. That's where she used to work programming computers till a month ago. She worked up till the last week before Jory was born. She's worked for the two years she and Steve have been married, supporting them while Steve goes to medical school.

She nearly jumped out of her skin when I dumped my books on the table. "Oh, Wendy. I didn't hear you come in. You scared me. I was so busy organizing this refrigerator so I can put Jory's food in it. Look, I put all the salad dressing bottles on the shelf in the door. How could you find them before?"

"Call them and they'll come to you," I said. I'm quick with one-liners.

That was my beginning with Marissa, and my worst fears were coming true. Not even here one day and she was organizing. I thought of the weekend I once spent with Marissa and Steve at their college residence. Marissa had this wall calendar with every appointment marked on it—color-coded. Red for household, blue for school-related, green for work-related, and purple for personal dates. She is the kind of person who has her hair cut the first Tuesday of each month.

"Why is the baby crying?" I asked, heading in toward the bedrooms.

"Don't bother him," Marissa said. "He's all right. He was just fed, burped, and changed. He's exercising his lungs."

Don't bother him? I thought. Who's bothering who? Sounds more like he's bothering me.

"Can't I even say hello to my own nephew?" I asked.

"I'd rather you didn't. I think he's going to fall asleep any minute now," she answered, closing the refrigerator and wiping the door handle.

"You don't have to wipe your fingerprints off everything you touch around here, Marissa. You live here. You're not a thief," I said, plopping down on a kitchen chair.

I guess that was as close as I could get to welcoming her. Then I thought, But she did kind of steal my favorite brother away from me when they got married two years ago.

She tried to be friendly, too. "Want a carob cupcake?" she asked. "I baked them. They taste just like chocolate chips only they're much healthier."

"You moved in and you had time to bake?" I said.

"There's not much to move from a college residence. A couple of friends helped me. Anyway, it's amazing what you can get done if you're organized."

She handed me what looked like a moon muffin and tasted like pancake mix when you add too much flour. Only it had chips of brown chalk masquerading as chocolate. "Thanks," I said.

"How are they?" She was fool enough to ask.

"What can I say?" I answered, feeling she could interpret that anyway she wanted. Then in an effort to be friendly I asked, "Want to watch *General Hospital* with me?"

"You don't watch that garbage, do you? Soaps at

your age? Wendy, you should put your mind to better use." And she even clicked her tongue at me.

"So don't," I said, tossing the moon muffin in the garbage. "I don't need anyone grading my likes and dislikes." I took the box of Oreos from the cabinet and poured myself a glass of milk. I took my snack into the living room, calling over my shoulder, "If you can tear yourself away from the intrigue of the salad dressings why don't you see why your baby is crying. I'd have checked on him by now." I felt glad that first of all, photos don't really cry. And second, that Gary had the babies' photos to worry about tonight and not me. I had enough on my hands right here, and I didn't want to miss another crisis moment on *General*. Marissa followed me into the living room.

"Where's Mom?" I asked, remembering she'd said she was taking the day off.

"I'm not supposed to tell you," Marissa said. "It's a surprise."

Oh no, I thought. Not another surprise that she wants to see my reaction to herself. But at least I didn't have to show her my latest detention slip and listen to a lecture before getting her to sign it . . . not yet, anyway. I added the paper to the pile of mail on the table. Marissa glanced at it as if it was her business.

"Not another detention, Wendy?" she said. "Your mother was telling me you've had a few already. She's worried about you."

"Talking about me behind my back," I muttered as she walked out of the living room.

"How long is that baby going to cry like that?" I

35.

called after Marissa. It was really getting on my nerves. I kept turning the TV up louder and louder.

"Turn down the sound," Marissa said. "It'll keep the baby up."

"Turn down the baby," I called back. "I was living here first."

After *General* I was doing my homework when the phone rang. It was Gary.

"We have to do the baby log," he said. "Want to split it? I'll do Askhim. You do Spot. Okay?"

"Okay," I said. "Even when you take a project seriously you can still be funny some of the time. Right?"

"Right. We'll do the work, read the chapters, research the facts and all. We can work for an A and still have some fun," Gary agreed.

"Sounds good to me," I said. "Where are the babies now?"

"Well, Askhim is at the ballet and Spot is on top of the refrigerator."

"I don't think I want to hear anymore."

"Okay," he said, and we hung up.

"The ballet?" I said out loud. "What is he talking about?"

I was headed for my room and I heard Marissa go into the bathroom and lock the door. So I tiptoed into Alan's room—which in one day my mother, the miracle worker, had turned into a nursery. There were no longer girlie calendars or rock star posters on the walls, and the bean bag chair was gone. She'd covered one entire wall with Snoopy and Peanuts patterned sheets stapled to the molding and half a matching curtain was already up on the window. The crib was in one corner and a changing table and chest of drawers were in the other.

The baby was very quiet now. I reached into the crib and put my hand on his little back to make sure he was breathing. I suppose Marissa knew best. She'd probably researched babies crying in some book, but it seemed so mean to let a tiny baby cry itself to sleep.

I remember crying myself to sleep a few times, once when my kitten died and once when I'd had a fight with my parents and decided they didn't love me. It was awful. How do we know what babies think and feel? I wanted very much to bend over the railing and kiss Jory on the fuzzy spot on the back of his neck. I was leaning way over the crib when I heard the bathroom door open and the click of high heels on the tile hallway headed my way.

Why was my heart pounding? Why did I feel like a criminal? All I was doing was adoring my own baby nephew and thinking maybe it wouldn't be so bad with the baby around, when Marissa came into the room and made a disgusted face. Then she beckoned with her finger, its long, perfectly filed, and pink-polished nail directing me to step outside the room.

I did and she laid her icy hand on my shoulder. "Let's get one thing straight, kiddo," she said. "You're not to go into the baby's room without my permission. Got it?"

"Got it," I said. "But that's Alan's room. Got it?" And I stormed into my bedroom and slammed the door. The baby started crying.

No, this was definitely not going to work out.

37.

4.

I SAT CURLED up on my bed, surrounded by my zoo of assorted-size stuffed animals. I love my room. I love the way my bed has bolsters to turn it into a couch during the day. I love my stereo and tapes, my makeup mirror and nail polish collection. I love the mess of books and clothes and papers. I love the purple mini-blinds on the window that match the purple in my wallpaper. I decorated the room all myself. I guess it shows who I am. At least my room is still my room—untouched by Marissa Incorporated, organizational expert.

I read the chapters on infancy and sat wondering if Gary wrote about Askhim in our baby log and if he'd come up with anything funny. I was reaching for my phone to call him when this horrible odor started seeping in through the crack under my bedroom door. I opened the door and called to Marissa. "What is that awful smell?"

She called back a one-word answer. "Dinner." I slammed the door and stuffed the crack with socks.

I figured the smell could very well be cauliflower, the grossest food there is. I never eat cauliflower. I don't even like to look at cauliflower. Not only does it smell bad, it looks like a plate of brains. Between the strong smell and the heat, (I swear Marissa must have turned the thermostat up to eighty degrees when she gave Jory a bath) I was beginning to feel dizzy.

I wished my parents would get home already. Maybe once they saw the heating bill Marissa was likely to run up, they'd see this living arrangement wouldn't work. Where were they, anyway? I glanced at the clock radio on my night table. It was six-thirty. I went into the kitchen to ask Marissa more about my missing parents. She was very mysterious about why they were late. "You'll see," she told me. "Your mother wants to surprise you."

"I hope she does better than the last surprise," I said.

"What was that?" Marissa attempted to sound interested.

"You," I answered, and leaned back against the wallpapered kitchen wall.

At first she sucked in such a deep breath that when she sighed and let it out, it kind of propelled her across the room like a balloon blown up but let go without a knot in it. She kind of zigzagged back and forth from the spice cabinet over the stove to the table. She'd been filling up the salt and pepper shakers that in all my life I don't ever remember seeing more than one-quarter full. I wondered if she counted the grains as she poured so they'd be exactly even. Then she drooped like a balloon with the air all out and said, "What would you have wanted for a surprise?"

"One of the stray dogs that was advertised on TV all this month on the 'won't you adopt this dog ad' for the

39.

ASPCA," I answered honestly. My mother once said that honesty is my best quality—and my worst. She said I could always be trusted and that this was very important to her since I was on my own a lot. But she said that I could also be trusted to embarrass the daylights out of her and tell someone loudly and publicly that their slip is hanging out, or their fly is open, or that their expensive new fur jacket "looks like dead cat." She said I have to learn to be discreet. I told her that first I have to learn what the word "discreet" means.

Marissa did not look thrilled that I preferred a stray dog to her, but she didn't say anything else because the baby was crying.

"Want me to check on him?" I offered.

"No, I'll do it," she said. So I went back to my room, closed the door, and worked on my baby log some more. I was thinking that maybe my parents were really sorry that they'd dumped Marissa, Steve, and Jory on me to turn my nice perfect world upside down. Maybe right this minute they were out trying to find that dog I wanted. My thoughts were interrupted by the telephone. I answered using the extension phone in my room. It was my mom.

"Hi, babe," she said. "Listen, Daddy and I are going to be a little later than we thought. We've run into a lot of traffic on the Belt Parkway because of . . ."

"What?" I said as a loud noise of a passing jet plane drowned out her voice.

"I'm calling from a phone booth at a gas station near the airport. There's probably a big puddle ahead that's slowed everything up. This parkway always floods out. Tell Marissa to go ahead with dinner without us. It's so nice to know you're not alone."

"But I liked being alone," I said.

"Try to make this work," she said. "I've racked my brain. I'm trying as best I can to do what's right for everyone in the family. Wait till you see the surprise we're bringing you. I think it will help." A truck rattled and roared by, and Mom shrieked, "This is crazy. I can't hear myself think. Bye," and hung up. I hung up, also. Then, sinking back on my bed against three pillows, I pushed my stuffed animal collection to the side. I felt a little better. At least she'd "racked her brain," whatever that means. I think I need a Mom-to-English dictionary. I checked the time. What were they doing out on Long Island at six-forty-five on a weekday evening? Maybe they had to go to a kennel out there. I hoped.

The doorbell rang and Marissa called. "Wendy—could you get that? It must be Steve or your folks. I'm elbow deep in A and D ointment—Jory's got a diaper rash."

I opened my door and as I walked by the cauliflower-smelly kitchen and dining room to the foyer, I held my nose. I looked through the peephole in the front door and called, "Who's there?" like I'm reminded to do at least forty times a week. I stared into the sparkling blue eyes of my brother, Steve. He's a big tease but funny enough to get away with it.

"I'm the vampire—come to suck your blood," he answered.

I opened the door and reached up to hug him. He's

about six feet tall. He scooped me up in his big arms and swung me around like he's always done ever since I was really little, then put me down. He was all wet from the rain.

"I feel like a vampire after working in the hematology lab all day," he said. "Um." He sniffed the air. "Cauliflower."

Steve and I are very different when it comes to foods and looks. He's blond like my father and I'm dark like my mom and we never like the same things to eat.

"You mean brains," I muttered. I didn't know if he heard.

"Is that my Jory baby I hear? Where's my beautiful Marissa?"

Beautiful Marissa? They'd probably be kissing and hugging and who knows what all the time and I'd have to listen to it, I thought, following him and remembering. Before Marissa and Jory came along, Steve used to call me "beautiful," or, "baby," like the time he was gently cleaning my skinned knees when I fell while I was learning to roller-skate on the rough sidewalk. He could even make peroxide poured onto a wound feel good. For a minute I wished Marissa and Jory would both disappear so just Steve would live here again. But that made me feel guilty because I love babies, especially my first and only baby nephew. So, instead, I just wished Marissa would disappear.

When I told Marissa my folks had said for us to eat without them, she said, "Darn, by the time they get here my special chicken cheese roll-ups will be dried out."

At dinner Steve portioned out the cauliflower pantomiming brain surgery, saying things like, "The frontal lobe for Wendy," and placing it on my plate next to my chicken cheese roll-up glop.

Jory cried all during dinner. Steve and Marissa took turns going in to him. "Why don't you just bring him out and let him join us? Maybe he's hungry," I suggested. In my health class textbook, I'd just been reading about why a baby cries, but Marissa gave me a "what do you know?" kind of look. Then she explained that according to Dr. Pepper Feinback, a world-famous pediatrician, a baby must learn to adapt to the society in which it lives and fit into the schedules of the parents. I never got past the doctor's name, I was laughing so hard.

"Dr. Pepper Feinback?" I sputtered a fine spray of gross-tasting chicken cheese roll-ups as I laughed. "Sounds more like a famous soda to me. Does she dance around her office singing"—and I got up and jumped around—"'I'm a Pepper, you're a Pepper, wouldn't you like to be a Pepper too? Dr. Pepper. Drink Dr. Pepper'?"

Marissa said two words to me, "Grow up!" and stormed out of the room.

Steve couldn't help chuckling, but he strode out after Marissa trying to calm her down, saying, "It's just a joke, sweetheart. Wendy has a crazy sense of humor. You just have to get used to it."

The problem with Marissa is she has *no* sense of humor. I hadn't really meant to upset her—not this time, anyway. So I cleaned up the dishes (no one had noticed that I didn't eat any cauliflower) and wiped the table. I was about to go into what until this morning had been my sister Kerry's room. Okay, so it was Steve's old room too, but Kerry had used it for the past four years. It seemed strange that now it was Steve and Marissa's room. I was going in to tell Marissa I'd cleaned up for her, when the phone rang. It was Gary.

"Askhim's asking for Mommy," he said. "I'll put him on." Gary changed his voice to a high pitch and said, "I want my mama." It's funny. I don't know why, but those words, even joking around, from Gary yet, made my heart stir.

"I wish I could be with you, too," I said, sounding the way my mother does when I call her at her office on days I'm sick in bed. On those days she's left my medicine lined up and a list of instructions and a thermos of chicken noodle soup for my lunch. This was silly. It was only pretend. I changed the subject. "Gary, did you do the log for Askhim?" I said, getting down to business.

"Yeah. That's why I called. I couldn't wait to tell you what I wrote. This project is really growing on me." Then I heard a crash and a moan in the background, and Gary said with a deep, serious, sad voice I'd never heard before, "Uh-oh—oh, no. I gotta go," and hung up. There was something going on in Gary's life that wasn't funny, it seemed to me. But what?

I didn't get to give it much thought because the doorbell rang. I crossed my fingers, hoping it would be my parents bringing me my very own adopted dog, and raced to the door.

My mouth hung open. It was a surprise, all right, and it was furry-looking too, but it was not a dog. Standing at the door was my grandma Minnie from

Florida, in her black fur-trimmed coat. There were a lot of suitcases being brought in by my father and mother. Grandma carried only her big tan pocketbook and overloaded, ready-to-explode plastic shopping bags, one from the Atlantic Federal Bank of Fort Lauderdale, and the other marked, THE MEAT BOUTIQUE.

She stood there clicking her tongue and looking at me. "Look how you've grown. Like a weed," she said, "no not a weed—a beautiful flower, like a gladiola maybe." She put down the bags and reached her arms out, and as if she was a vacuum cleaner I was sucked up into them. The fur from her big collar tickled my nose, and as much as I love my grandma Minnie and the delicious smell of her Shalimar perfume, all I could think of was the piece of fur on my tongue. I freed myself from her tight squeeze, picked the hair off my tongue, then hugged her as hard as I could. I kissed her soft, soggy cheeks and ran my fingers through her blond, short hair. It was soft and silky. My grandma does not believe in hair spray.

Grandma was here to save me from Marissa, I thought to myself. She heard I needed her and she came right away. I was deep in these thoughts when Grandma said, "So now, where's that cutest baby in the world?"

"I'm right here," I started to say, but swallowed the last word as Grandma continued.

"A great-grandchild in this very house. When I heard that, I was on the phone to Delta Airlines in minutes." Then she bustled past me, heading for the bedrooms, Jory, and Marissa. A funny feeling wriggled through my stomach like the kind of feeling you get when a test paper is handed out and you expected to do well but you didn't. I'd always been the cutest baby in the world.

Mom and Dad looked bedraggled and weary after carrying in three suitcases, two cartons, a bag of oranges and a box of coconut patties. Even Dad's new mustache was dripping from the rain, and it felt yucky when he kissed me. "So, Wendy," Dad said, "one thing for sure, today you can't say nothing ever happens around here." Something told me my father didn't sound overwhelmed with joy. Overwhelmed, yes. Joy, no.

Mom was all over me, hugging and cheerful. "See, now you won't have to feel like a baby-sitter and you won't be alone with Marissa bossing you around. See, baby. I do listen to you. I thought about what you said before you stormed out this morning. I know this isn't easy on you. It's not easy on us either. So the best I could think of was to call Grandma and see if she wanted to help us out. Grandma to the rescue. I figure, what's one more? You cook for six or you cook for seven, it makes no difference. I just wish I had one-quarter of Grandma's energy. That's all. So what do you think of my surprise?" Mom asked the fatal question. She didn't expect the honest answer that popped out of my mouth.

"You know I love Grandma Minnie. And I love you for trying—but it would have been much simpler if your surprise had been that stray dog," I said, and my eyes welled up with tears. My mom put her hands on my shoulders.

"Wendy, I am trying my best. We will all just have to adapt. It's an important part of life," Mom said, talking her own language again. I was thinking more of independence than adaptation. How can I become independent—give myself independence lessons—how can I be me—with all these people arriving to take over my life!

5.

I DIDN'T SLEEP much last night, not just because Mom and Dad had been upset and before signing my detention slip had given me a lecture on behaving in school. And not just because I was worrying about my baby photos, hoping Gary, the clown, was taking good care of them. And also not just because Jory cried every four hours. I didn't sleep because Grandma Minnie snores something fierce. I think the windows even rattled from the vibration. Sometimes when she exhaled, the top curl of her dyed blond hair unfurled like one of those noisemakers you blow into on New Year's Eve. I stared at the curl for hours waiting for it to straighten out again. I could see clearly because Grandma insisted on having a night-light on in the room so if she had to get up to go to the bathroom during the night she wouldn't, as she put it, "break her neck over the clutter of sneakers, magazines, and whatever" on the floor in my room. She also said that I would have till tomorrow night to clean up.

Mom thought Grandma would sleep on the cot she'd put up in Jory's room, but Marissa wouldn't hear of having Grandma disturbed every few hours or so, and

Grandma said a cot was bad for her back. So, guess whose room Marissa suggested Grandma sleep in? After all, it does have a high-rise bed in it.

When I was little it was a treat to sleep with Grandma. My brothers and sister and I would fight over who would get her. She'd tickle our arms till we fell asleep, and it felt so good. Last night she just said good-night, and when I said good-night I woke her up. That's how fast she fell asleep. She was up early, too. She and Marissa had breakfast all ready for everyone. I can't complain about that. Pancakes on a weekday morning with melted butter to pour over them so you don't even have to wait for the butter to soak in. And there was syrup oozing over the top. The odor was thick in the air, mixing with the aroma of perking coffee. It was like a scene for a TV commercial.

Only Steve didn't have time to eat. "I have to race," he said. "I have death and doughnuts this morning." That's what he calls his early-morning pathology class. He has this cadaver he works on. He named it Charlie. Steve and all the other med students in his class bring coffee and a doughnut and eat breakfast as they listen to their professor describe the part of the body they'll be cutting up to see how the disease affected it. Talk about gross!

Grandma made a fuss and practically followed him out the door waving a pancake and muttering, "He's too thin. He's working too hard. He needs to eat a good breakfast and get energy. How will he become a doctor if he doesn't eat breakfast?"

My father laughed. "I wish it was as simple as that,"

49.

he said. "Breakfast is cheap. It's med school that can break the bank. Right, Marissa?" Dad smiled at Marissa, but Marissa, who had helped with the payments until recently, didn't smile back. She looked as if her feelings had been hurt. Then Dad said, "I'm joking, Marissa." But I don't think he was.

Everything else went okay except for the coffee-maker incident and the syrup argument.

"Mom," my father said to his mother-in-law. "Why don't you use the coffee-maker I bought Susan last Chanukah? You set it to the time you want it to brew the coffee and push the button."

"You must have had to dig in the closet for that old Pyrex percolator," Mom added as Grandma poured another cup of coffee from it.

"I like to make real coffee in the morning, not electric, and that thing with all the dials and buttons I wouldn't touch," Grandma said. "I'm not an engineer." Then she changed the subject. "Anyway, how come you use Vermont Maid and not Aunt Jemima syrup?" She asked Mom the question as if accusing her of a crime. "We always used Aunt Jemima."

"Douglas's side of the family always used Vermont Maid," Mom answered, glancing at my dad. "He likes it better."

But the syrup incident really became a crisis moment when Grandma gave Jory a taste of syrup on her finger. She dipped her finger in it and let him lick it off. Marissa went wild. She grabbed Jory and started out of the room screaming, "You don't feed an infant food that has preservatives like sodium benzoate and sorbic acid from an unsterilized finger! An infant who hasn't even had his shots yet. Don't you know anything about babies? If only I'd been able to nurse him!"

Grandma looked crushed.

Ours was definitely not going to be like the Ingalls family on *Little House on the Prairie.* I thought Marissa might come back and hit Grandma over the head with the Dr. Pepper Feinback book. I hate violence, so I got an early start for school. On my way out I heard Grandma call to Mom, "Susan, don't you have a dishrag? How do you clean dishes around here?"

What is a dishrag? I wondered.

"Use the dishwasher," Mom called back.

"For so few dishes you're going to waste electricity? What's the big deal to wash a few plates?" was Grandma's answer. I closed the door behind me before I heard Mom's reply. It was strange to me to hear my mother spoken to as if she were a teenager.

I was the first at the lamppost and Robby Marshall was the second once again. As he handed me the baby cribs he'd made for Spot and Askhim, our hands touched. I looked right into his blue eyes. For a minute I didn't even think or care about Marissa, Jory, and all the hassle.

"Aren't they beautiful?" he said. For a second I thought he meant my eyes, but he meant the cribs he'd just built.

"They sure are," I answered. "Excellent."

Then I noticed he wasn't looking into my eyes anymore, he was looking down at my pocketbook and I got embarrassed, remembering I now owed him two dol-

51.

lars. After rummaging in my change purse, I came up with four quarters. "Gary will give you the rest," I said, then looked around, wishing Brenda and Jennifer would walk faster. I could see them up the block and I waved. You could hear the car horns as impatient morning traffic was building up at the traffic light on Ocean Parkway a few blocks away.

"Let me show you how to use the crib so it won't break. Come closer," he said, and put his hand on my shoulder to kind of guide me the couple of steps toward him. I could feel his touch even through my sweatshirt and sweater jacket. "You have to be real careful when you lower the railing. Just push up the paper-clip hinges gently," Robby instructed. I would have known that without his explaining everything like Marissa does, but I listened as if it was news to me. I even practiced. "Good," he said, "you got it." All this would have been romantic if only this old man wasn't walking his dog nearby, trying to get it to go at the curb and not on the grass. I was hoping it wouldn't go at all.

It seemed almost as if Brenda gave me a dirty look when she and Jennifer joined us. I got this peculiar feeling that she was trying to make me look dumb and herself smart. "That's easy," she said, taking the cribs out of my hands and fiddling with the balsa wood and paper-clip miniature rails. "You're so talented, Robby," she added, "I'm glad you're *my* partner." Robby beamed, and that was the end of my conversation with him.

Jennifer hadn't said a word. This must be so tough

on her—not having a photo baby anymore. Mrs. Devin was firm on not giving second chances when it came to baby-safety errors. "Want to carry Spot when I get her back from Gary? He had both photos at his house last night. Mothers of twins need lots of help," I told her.

"Sure," she said, "and I won't let Sherman Barker near her." We all started walking. I didn't feel like talking about the changes going on at my house—not with Robby walking with us. But then Jennifer asked me, "How come your phone was busy all evening. I mean till late at night. I called and called." That's when I realized Marissa must have taken the phone off the hook so the baby wouldn't be disturbed. Now that's where I draw the line. Phone calls are my life!

"You wouldn't believe what is going on at my house. Just two days ago all I had to contend with was a working mother and a father growing a mustache. Now there's a baby nephew crying all night, a sister-in-law who is so organized that groceries are now lined up in size order and towels are alphabetized, and a grandmother who uses dishrags, saves electricity, and follows you around with a Dustbuster to catch crumbs. And my mother walks around talking baby talk to Jory one minute, and the next she talks to him as if he's an infant art major. 'You and I will go to museums,' she says. 'I'll show you Renoirs and Mary Cassatt paintings.' My father, on the other hand, talks to him in a Donald Duck voice, saying, 'Smile for Grandpa.' Now I ask you, is this normal?"

"Sounds great!" Jennifer said.

53.

I don't know why I bothered to go on. Jennifer is an only child. She thinks being part of a big family is great. She's never understood when I've had any problems with my family. I've loved being part of my family, but even great families have problems. I listen and sympathize when Jennifer has troubles. "I feel like an intruder in my own house—like I'm in the way. And everyone wants to tell me what to do or not to do. My brother eats breakfast in a morgue. And now I find out I can't even get my phone calls because the phone's off the hook! I can't take much more of this."

I had only started to explain when Gary arrived with a loud voice that could be heard even though fire engines were going by on the avenue. He was racing to catch up with us and shouted words like a news flash, the way I sometimes do. I'd never heard anyone else do that.

"Photo of infant takes first steps—more at eleven," Gary said. He has a way of making people laugh. Even Jennifer, who doesn't laugh easily, has mentioned to me that she likes it that Gary walks with us because he's fun to be with. But Brenda thinks he's too silly for us, that we've outgrown him. Lately I think she thinks everyone is silly except her.

I was dying to ask about last evening's phone conversation: the moaning and crashing sounds, then his panicked voice. But now wasn't the time. Brenda and Robby did most of the talking. I did ask Gary to explain about Askhim going to the ballet last night. He said he'd put the photo into his mom's pocketbook before she went to Lincoln Center.

"I think the kid is going to be a dancer," he said. "I wanted him to have a cultural experience. The textbook says babies can appreciate music at an early age."

I wondered if Gary liked to dance like I do. I pretended Askhim got his talent from me and I felt proud. I also wished I was alone in my house so I could dance around freely, right now. We walked the few blocks further to school, and Gary handed me the babies, cups and all. I was still balancing the cribs on top of my books. He helped me open the heavy door. "You don't want to end up with a pile of splinters instead of cribs," he said.

A couple of kids laughed, and Gary looked happy— as if he could face the day better with laughter as a vitamin. "Thanks," I said.

Jennifer took Spot to carry with her today. As we passed the office, Gary stuck his head in the doorway and said to the secretary, "I'll be in gym for an hour. Hold all my calls." Then he raced down the hall.

In homeroom, a room that has eighty-two layers of turquoise paint and is still peeling, there was this dumb announcement about bathrooms. Mrs. Barnett, our principal, has apparently just found out about the smoking that everyone knows goes on in certain bathrooms. Even the little sixth graders know to wait till they get home to go rather than use the smoky school bathrooms and risk getting into trouble.

Mrs. Barnett, between microphone squeals, announced over the PA. system, "For better supervision, on even periods you may use odd-numbered bathrooms. On odd periods go to even bathrooms."

"Now you have to take notes to see where you can go to the bathroom," I said out loud, and the kids around me started to laugh.

In third period, English, we had a substitute. She had a black kinky perm on her little head, a thin body, and big hips. She was very pale, petal white, as if she might faint any minute, but her lipstick was bright red.

All the kids were talking and fooling around and she thought that by clearing her throat, going "Ahem, ahem, ahem" she'd get our attention. Now, in a situation like this you have to get dramatic and pull a window shade up and let it snap back with a bang that makes everyone's heart jump. If I was her that's what I would have done.

She finally gave up coughing and wrote some words on the board, breaking each word into syllables and pronouncing each syllable slowly and clearly. One of the words was "as'–ter–oid." I don't laugh if a person uses the wrong word or mispronounces a word. Where I volunteer, at the nursing home, some of the older people I visit mix up words. I never laugh at them. But this substitute teacher was being so stuffy and didn't even know she'd said a word teachers don't usually say in class. I couldn't control my giggles. A lot of kids were chuckling. I, however, was roaring.

The substitute turned to me and said, "If you can't stop laughing, go to the back of the room and laugh. I don't want you interrupting the class."

"Okay," I said, and taking Askhim, in his crib (Jennifer had Spot with her), I walked to the back of the room, sat down, and howled.

My luck, this is when Miss Mannis, the assistant principal, walked in. Twenty-two kids are sitting in the front, one kid—me—is sitting in the back laughing. I swallowed a gulp of laughter as she pointed to me and mouthed, "Detention."

I was really relieved to get to fourth period, health—my friends and Mrs. Devin. At least Mrs. Devin has a sense of humor. She's quick. When Joshua Gruppman asked her, "Can I go to the bathroom?" she answered, "I don't know. Can you?" He looked at her like you wanted to say, "Earth to Joshua. Earth to Joshua." "You mean *may* I go to the bathroom," Mrs. Devin explained.

But I was quicker yet, adding, "Oh, you have to go to the bathroom, too, Mrs. D?"

"You got me this time," she said, and laughed.

Gary cracked up. He really appreciates a good joke.

"Take out your baby logs," she said, starting to walk down the first aisle, "and let's have a look."

"Hey, Brenda," I said. "How's it going?"

"Great. You should see the way Robby even wrote in calligraphy, 'Baby's first photo.'" Everyone was really impressed, including me. There was no end to Robby Marshall's talents. My baby photos looked snug and comfortable in the cribs he'd made. Once again I wished he was my partner.

Gary removed the photos from their cribs and put them in one of his pockets. Then he took out the baby log he'd made, which meant loose papers went flying and he had to chase after them, leaving a shoe print on one and half-crumpling another as he picked it up. I leaned over to see what he'd written just as he turned to say something to me. We were accidentally so close we were almost kissing. We moved away real fast, and I think he blushed.

Mrs. Devin gave us a lesson on how girls are brought up to be the caretakers but how it's as important for boys to know the fun and troubles of caretaking.

Mrs. Devin went on, "The way today's economy is, many families need two incomes. And there'd be less tension if people thought about when and why they want to have a baby, and if they can afford it. So, for tomorrow, read the textbook chapters about feeding and sleeping patterns, and prepare a budget of what it might cost to feed and clothe a baby and take care of its health needs during its first year."

Then Gary livened up the class and shocked me. He took one of our baby photos and started ripping it up, muttering, "This is a demonstration of child abuse."

I could feel my breath catch, as if a crisis moment was about to occur. I reached out to protect my baby photo as if it were real. The whole class seemed to be gasping and ready to pounce. I couldn't believe it— Gary just let the ripped pieces tumble onto the floor.

I bent down to the floor. My eyes were closed and I was shaking. I couldn't bear to look.

The only person who was laughing was Gary. And when he realized he was the only one, he stopped mid-chuckle.

I opened my eyes and looked up at him. His face got pale as he looked back at me and saw the tears welling up in my eyes. "Oh, Wendy, don't be upset. It's a joke. It's not Askhim. It's an imposter photo. Askhim's in my other pocket." Then he reached over and, in front of all these kids, he took me in his arms with the gentlest touch I ever felt and he rubbed my back and whispered soothingly, "I'm sorry. I thought it was funny." Then he handed me the real Askhim photo and ran out of the room.

6.

WITH THE SCENE I'd made and Gary's dramatic exit rerunning in my mind, I sat down at my desk stroking Askhim's image and trying not to hear what the other kids were whispering to each other. It sounded like a buzz to me. I couldn't look at the imposter scraps, and I was thankful when Jennifer picked them up off the floor and handed them to Mrs. Devin. I was so embarrassed. The whole class had seen my inside feelings. I never let anyone see them. I also hadn't seen Gary this upset since first grade, when he once got real mad at this kid, Howard, who had a Mickey Mouse wristwatch but always said the time was "quarter minutes to two."

"You don't say 'quarter minutes,'" he'd said. "And it can't always be a quarter to two! Dumb and stupid. Dumb and stupid." I can still remember him mumbling. I don't know why I remembered that now after all these years, but I just did.

I wondered where Gary went. If he left the school building he'd be in big trouble. I kept watching the door hoping he'd come back in, laughing the whole thing off, and making everything all right. That's what someone like Gary was supposed to do.

My whole life felt tossed in the air, and pieces were falling wherever they happened to fall. Nothing was the same as yesterday. I wasn't the same, my family had a population explosion, and now not even Gary was the same. I felt really angry at him. Gary had always meant fun and laughter. Never any troubles or worry or anger. I never realized before how much I needed that fun person. I wondered if we'd ever be real good friends again.

When Gary didn't come back in five minutes, I asked Mrs. Devin if I could go look for him.

"I was just about to suggest that," she said. "This isn't like Gary to get upset and stay out of class." She wrote out a pass and handed it to me.

I asked Jennifer to watch Askhim as well as Spot and I left the room. Everyone's staring made me trip over nothing but embarrassment. Then the door slammed, making the glass rattle.

The hallways are so empty during classes. You hear your own footsteps echo. It feels as if you're walking outside the world, glancing at everything going on below, like an astronaut circling the earth. I figured if I was the one who was upset, I'd run to the bathroom, and I wouldn't stop to figure out odd or even like we're supposed to. I'd run to the nearest one and splash cold water on my face or flush the toilet so no one would hear me sob. Great, so that meant here I was headed for the boys' bathroom at the end of the hall. I'd never been in a boys' bathroom, and I didn't know if I'd have the nerve to go in now.

First I just knocked on the door, but no one answered. So then I opened it a crack and whispered,

"Gary, are you in there?" Then I added, "Is anyone in there?" No answer. I opened the door a bit and looked in. Sinks lined one wall and urinals lined the other. Of course, I've seen pictures of them or maybe I'd seen them in kindergarten when boys and girls used the same bathroom, but now all I could think about was silly things like whether boys talk to each other while they're going. And if they turned to talk to the person next to them wouldn't they go all over them?

I was glad there was no one in the bathroom. Then, just as the door closed behind me, I heard the toilet flush in one of the stalls in the back of the room.

"Gary, I sure hope that's you," I said, getting this nervous feeling. "If it is, please come out. I'm not upset anymore, I'm worried about you." I didn't get to find out who was in there because at that moment the door was opened and I felt a poke of a finger in my back. I whirled around and was eye to eye with Miss Mannis.

"You again?" the assistant principal said. "Just what do you think you're doing and what were you saying?"

I was going to make up a story like I was walking by and I heard a cry for help and was going to answer it. But I figured if it was Gary in there I didn't want to get him into trouble, since he didn't have a pass. So I just played innocent and said, "I was just saying, 'Oops, wrong bathroom.' Sorry," showed her my pass, then clutched my stomach and doubled over with pretend cramps as I went into the girls' bathroom next door. Next thing I knew I heard a knock on the door. Probably Miss Mannis, I figured.

But then I heard, "Come out, come out, wherever you are." I sighed with relief, hearing Gary's voice.

I was so glad to hear him I dashed out pushing the door hard and practically smashing him against the wall as the door opened so fast.

"Whoa!" he said. "You want me to look like Gumby!" I cracked up at the thought of the rubber toy. He just took my hand and we started walking back to class as always. We weren't the same people as we'd been this morning but we were still friends. Maybe more than friends, even.

"I'm okay now," Gary said. "I'm very sorry I upset you. I didn't know how much this project meant to you. I thought it was just a good joke. Are you okay?"

"I'm fine," I said.

"I want you to be fine," he said very softly. And I felt this funny feeling deep inside my stomach. I never felt that before.

My thumb kind of stroked his thumb as we walked back to class. "Things are really tough at my house right now," he said.

"Mine, too," I said, but we didn't have time to say anything more. I pulled my hand out of his and we both went inside the classroom. Without even planning it, he bowed and I curtsied as if the whole entire scene had been an act. Then we went to our seats triumphantly to a round of applause from the kids. The crisis moment had passed.

Lunch was an unidentifiable object, floating in grease, that the lunchroom ladies chased with a spatula and slid onto a stale roll. They actually expected us to eat it. Gary told me he'd come over to my house around three-thirty and we'd work on the baby assignment that was due on Friday, just the day after tomorrow.

In French, my last class, Mrs. Smith has this "you must talk only in French" rule, which can turn into an emergency situation when you happen by accident to staple your finger instead of the paper, as I did, and you can't remember how to conjugate the verb to bleed. I stood there dripping red drops and saying "Je . . . je . . . je." I finally just said, "Je bleeding to death!" She got the message, gave in, and let me go to the nurse's office for a Band-Aid.

Gary didn't walk home with us today because he had to get something on the avenue. Sometimes he's very mysterious. I think I'll suggest we work at his house one of these days so I can see what's going on.

Brenda and Robby are getting along so well that I think Brenda's forgotten that she has two best friends. Jennifer and I ended up walking together and keeping our distance since Brenda kept giving these looks like, "Get out of the way."

I psyched myself up for reentry into the three-ring circus that had once been my home. It felt odd and not really very good to ring the doorbell and know someone would answer it and that the someone might very well be Marissa. I still wore my key on its string around my neck, but my finger was throbbing from the French staple, so the bell was easier to manage.

What I totally didn't expect was that the three-ring circus had turned into four rings, or rather into a war zone. Things were sure changing fast around here. The door was opened. At first all I saw was a hairy arm.

Definitely not Marissa. And one place Grandma wasn't furry was her arm. Steve was at school and has no dark hairs on his arms anyway. And Jory certainly didn't creep out of his crib to answer the bell and turn into a hairy thing. It wasn't my mother or father. So who was it? Now, with a full house, a burglar was going to arrive on the scene? Then I heard the lovable bellow that is unmistakable to me.

"What, are you gonna stand out there till frost sets in and you become a snowman? Oy, wait a minute. Let me correct myself. Marissa, are you listening? I mean snowperson."

"Grandpa," I said, practically dropping my books in surprise as I came in and closed the door. "What are you doing here? And what's wrong with your arm that it's in a sling?"

"Don't drop those books on my foot, or I'm really sunk," he said, pushing an almost falling book back in place with his good hand. "What's wrong with my arm you ask? Your mother and father are making a minor mishap into a major tragedy. That's what's wrong with my arm."

"But you're wearing a sling and cast on your arm," I said, pointing.

"So an old man like me falls on the slippery leaves, breaks his wrist, and dislocates his shoulder. So what's the big deal?" Grandpa answered. "I never should have let that doctor call your father. How can you have confidence in a doctor named Seth who wears dungarees, looks like he's twelve years old, and calls me Lou. That was the big mistake, letting him phone your father. Next thing I know my big-shot son and your mother were at the hospital to pick me up. They imprison me here in this *meshuggeneh* household, which, pardon the expression, contains a blond Chef Boyardee from Florida, your mother's mother, who is at this very moment in the kitchen tangled up in the pasta machine, your sister-in-law Marissa, who has what to say about everything, and my beautiful great-grandson, who is being starved to death because it's not the right time. Now I ask you. You're a sensible kid. Is this any place for an old man to recuperate? I am trapped here until my cast can come off."

I hugged him and kissed his cheek. My Grandpa lives in a studio apartment a few miles away, and his nickname is "Grandpa—the mouth." I love to listen to his "verbal explosions," as my mother calls them. Finally someone understood how I felt. "Poor Grandpa," I said, gently patting the fingers sticking out of the plaster half-cast on his arm.

Then a thought crossed my mind. But where was he gonna sleep? Not only wouldn't it be cool to have my father's widowed father sleep with my mother's widowed mother, but they hate each other. This was beginning to feel like a scene from a picture book or a nursery rhyme. A modern-day version of the old woman who lived in a shoe, only instead of so many children she didn't know what to do, it was so many relatives I wouldn't know what to do. This is silly, but all I could think of was us all lining up to take showers tomorrow morning. We'd need tickets like at Stern's bakery on Avenue J.

"Lou!" Grandma called to Grandpa. "What are you doing up? You're supposed to be injured, so sit down already. Don't be such a big shot. I made you tea. It will make you feel better."

"I hate tea," Grandpa roared. "Tea is for sick people. I'm not sick. I'm injured."

"I made tea for you—you drink it!" Grandma said, walking into the living room and putting a tray down on the coffee table so hard the tea made a wave in the cup. Then she walked back to the foyer where I stood with Grandpa, grabbed his good wrist, and Grandpa, grimacing and towering over Grandma, momentarily gave in and let her lead him to the rose-colored sofa and prop his arm up on an embroidered pillow.

The baby was screaming. I found Marissa in her room crying. Mom and Dad were, of course, away at work. And here I was—me and my baby photos—home sweet home.

7

I SHOUTED A general hello "to whom it may concern," and headed for my room, at least half of which was my one last stronghold. But not even that was the same. I looked around our shared bedroom, barely recognizing it. Grandma had straightened both her side and mine. My shoes were no longer scattered around the room or under the bed. They were now lined up neatly in a shoe bag that hung on the closet door. Some of my shoes had these wooden feet in them. It really looked gross.

There was no longer a rainbow of sweaters and blouses hanging on my desk chair, and no pile of books and folders on its seat. I sat down on it for the first time in months, then reached for the glass of water where yesterday's wad of bubble gum should have been floating. But the glass was clean, dry, and empty except for a tube of Poli-Grip Grandma must use for her false teeth.

The beds were neatly made and my stuffed animals were arranged in size order on my pillow, which made me suspicious that Marissa had something to do with this, too.

Jory screamed, and Grandma called, "Marissa, I'll

get the baby. You rest. You'll feel better after a little sleep. You were up half the night with him. No wonder you're in tears."

A weary-sounding Marissa answered, "Thanks, Grandma."

"Wendy, come have some milk and cookies," Grandma called. "I baked oatmeal cookies. Oatmeal is good for you."

Grandma was taking over and I didn't like it one bit. What I wanted was my box of Oreo cookies, some soda, and my spot in the living room to watch *General Hospital* till Gary got here. I knew Grandpa wouldn't mind if I joined him in the living room.

Oh no. Gary. What would he think of this madhouse? He'd probably run out of here screaming. That's what I felt like doing, but I controlled myself, determined to make this miserable moment into an independence lesson. I would confront Grandma calmly and assert my rights to my room—that if I want my half messy, it's my right to have it messy.

But when I walked into the kitchen I didn't get to say a word. She handed Jory over to me and said, "Hold this poor little boy." Then she whispered, "The poor baby is being starved to death by a book. If Dr. Pepper Feinback only drank formula for three weeks, she'd be up all night crying, too."

The fight for my independence was put on hold as I took Jory in my arms. Finally I was cuddling my very own nephew, and it felt so good. He was warm and soft and smelled like Johnson's baby powder and lotion. I made sure to support his neck and head with my hand, the way I'd read in my child-care book—babies that young can get hurt if they snap their head back. His head felt so soft and fuzzy, and I ran my lips over his baby-fine hair, then kissed him. I patted his back and turned my body from side to side to rock him, but he kept on crying.

"He'll stop crying in a minute," Grandma said. She poured something into his baby dish, covering the Peter Rabbit design on the bottom up to its ears. Then she added heated formula and stirred.

"What are you doing?" I asked.

"I'm making him some baby oatmeal. You'll see. He'll sleep through the night. This is my only chance. Marissa watches me like a hawk."

The thought of a quiet night sounded good to me. In my child-care book it said to start your baby on solid food by the third week, so I didn't think it would hurt Jory to have oatmeal. Anyway, Marissa had told Grandma oatmeal was good for you.

"Marissa will shoot you if she finds out," I said. "You know that, of course. She only listens to Dr. Pepper Feinback."

"So, if she'll shoot me, she'll shoot me," Grandma answered. "And how many grandchildren does Dr. Pepper Whatever have? Me, I've got four and this great grandson." She put a dab of the pasty mixture on her wrist. "Too hot. Walk with him a bit to calm him down before Marissa comes running."

I carried Jory into the living room and turned on *General Hospital*, bending at the knees and bracing his head with part of my arm like the diagram in my book.

"Turn the TV set up louder," Grandpa said, from

the couch, "so I can hear it over the howling of my starving great-grandchild."

I kept rubbing Jory's back and walking around the room. He seemed to like the light from the TV, or maybe he's going to be a doctor like his father, because I swear he calmed down and started to watch *General* with Grandpa and me.

Twice Grandma yelled in, "Answer the doorbell."

And I called back, "It's on TV. The doorbell rings a lot on *General*." But the next time Grandma called, it really was the doorbell. Uh-oh— Gary, I thought, just as Jory started to scream again.

Grandma was calling, "Bring Jory in, the you-know-what's cooled off." I peered through the peephole, still a latchkey kid habit, and opened the door quickly, carefully balancing Jory in a position where his head wouldn't snap backward.

"Come in," I called to Gary, backing off so Jory wouldn't get a draft. Mrs. Devin had mentioned that in her talk on care of the newborn.

Gary walked in, took one look at me and Jory, and his mouth opened wide. He did one of his instant faint numbers, slithering slowly to the floor. Then he stretched out at my feet, opened one eye, and said, "I don't believe it! Look what's developed. You turned a photo into a baby!"

Grandpa, the mouth, watched this whole scene, then said, "Come on, whoever you are on the floor over there. I'll move over. Join the crowd. Minnie! Make another cup of tea." Jory was screaming. Grandma was calling me. Grandpa was muttering lines like, "A zoo. A definite zoo they bring me to recover in. *Meshugge*."

71.

All I could think of to do in the midst of this chaos was say, "Grandpa, this is my friend Gary. Gary, this is my grandpa Lou Meyer."

Gary, to my surprise, got up, then smoothed out his shirt and unzipped his jacket while walking across the room. "How do you do, sir?" he said, and shook Grandpa's good hand.

"How do I do is not the question. How do I don't do is what I want to know."

"Come on, Gary," I said. "Grandma's calling."

Gary took off his jacket, hung it on the doorknob, then followed me into the kitchen laughing. "So who is the baby—Askhim or Spot?" he said.

"My nephew Jory," I answered, "and my grandma's about to feed him his first solid food. We can observe grandparent/grandchild behavior and write it up in our baby log."

I gave Jory a dozen more kisses. "Can I kiss that soft spot on his head?" Gary asked. "It's my favorite place on babies."

"Sure," I said. "Just be gentle." And he was. "Grandma, this is my friend Gary. Gary, this is my grandma Minnie Sokel," I said as we walked into the kitchen.

"How do you do?" Gary was brave enough to try those words out again. I hoped he would get a normal answer. But Grandma first wiped her hand on her apron, then shook his hand.

"I do just fine—just watch and see." She took the baby from me, then sat down on a chair at the kitchen table, cradling Jory in her arms. From a tiny spoon she started to feed a bit of baby oatmeal into Jory's mouth.

He smacked his lips and the crying stopped as if he had an on/off switch. He occasionally sputtered, sending a spray of oatmeal all over us. Sometimes more oatmeal oozed out the sides of his mouth than went in. Gary, Grandma, and I were laughing. Once I looked around, and all of our mouths were moving as if each one of us was eating the oatmeal.

"You see, he was starving," Grandma said, adding, "and you kids must be hungry too. Eat those oatmeal cookies and drink some milk."

I offered the dish of cookies to Gary, and he took one and ate it with such enjoyment—almost as if he was feeling nourished for the first time, like Jory was. It was more than just eating food. There was a look of contentment on both their faces, as if they felt happy and cared for and weren't used to it. I offered Gary another cookie and stuck it in his mouth myself. We both laughed.

Grandpa walked in and, surveying the scene, said, "Minnie, that's the first smart thing I've seen you do all day. That baby was starving."

"From your grandpa, that, kids, is a compliment, believe it or not," Grandma explained.

Grandpa clucked over Jory, saying, "Now you look ready to handle a nice, juicy steak."

Grandpa said he was hungry, and I got him a hard-boiled egg from the bowl on the bottom shelf of the refrigerator, and he showed me how to crack it, roll it around in my hand, and peel it so the shell came off easily.

"Even with one arm in a sling you have to keep doing for yourself." Then he added, "So what's new with you, kiddo?"

I explained about the baby project. "It's to help us to be better parents and to think about when and if we should have kids."

"We never had time to learn how to bring up children," Grandma said. "We made our mistakes. But what we did have were parents and aunts around us to lend a hand. That poor Marissa thinks she has to handle every decision on her own. Superwoman she isn't. With her parents living all the way across the country in California, she can't even afford to call her mother for advice. You hear me, Lou, we have to help that girl."

"I hear you. I hear you. You never stop talking," Grandpa bellowed. But even his bellow didn't awaken Jory, who'd been burped, and was now sleeping soundly in Grandma's arms.

Gary and I went into the living room to write up our baby log and research the cost factors of bringing up babies.

I was kind of hoping Gary would have gone home before Marissa got up and discovered the oatmeal dish and spoon. Grandma didn't want to sneak around, she'd said. She wanted Marissa to see the baby needs the cereal. So she'd left the oatmeal in the baby dish and on the spoon. I didn't want Gary to hear Marissa's hysterics. I was sure he must think things crazy enough, already.

We phoned a baby-clothing store to find out the price of a layette, the little shirts, kimonos, and blankets babies wear in the beginning. When I explained the project to the woman who answered the phone, and told her we needed cost figures for the first year of a baby's life, she told me to hang on while she got a recent issue of *New York Magazine* that had an article called "The High Cost of Baby Booming." She read off the amounts to me, and I repeated them to Gary, who wrote them down.

"For the upwardly mobile child, first-year costs add up to $27,677.52. That includes getting started, necessities, room and clothing, child care, safety measures, equipment, first books, and milestone costs like cameras and film." I couldn't believe one stretchie outfit cost nine dollars.

As an excuse to get Gary home before Marissa got louder, I suggested we write the baby log about grandparents and babies separately and surprise each other tomorrow. We were saying good-bye when the screaming started.

"You what?" I heard Marissa shout. "Oh, Grandma. I don't believe you did that without asking me. Don't ever touch that baby again without my permission. Do you understand?"

It came to me at that moment that maybe Marissa was still fighting for independence like I was. And how could I come down on Grandma now, about my room, after Marissa had yelled at her like that? I'd have to wait a while longer.

"I'm sorry for all the excitement and confusion and stuff," I said, suddenly feeling shy with Gary.

"Don't worry about it," he said, taking his jacket off the door knob where he'd hung it. He put it on and zipped it. Then he patted my shoulder. "You don't know how lucky you are."

I wondered what he meant and decided that it was

time to find out more about Gary. Tomorrow I'd insist we work at his house.

"Oh, can I take Spot for the night?" he asked, and I got her from my room. Somehow I felt confident he'd take care of her.

I closed the door after him and listened to the chaos. In the background the adopt-a-dog commercial from the ASPCA was on the TV again, and I wished once more for a simple life. Just me and the real Spot, the dog I wanted to adopt.

8.

GRANDMA SERVED BROILED fish for dinner with that red stuff, paprika, on top. It didn't disguise it. The whole house smelled even worse than Marissa's cauliflower. Marissa was so upset with Grandma feeding Jory cereal that she refused to come out of her room. Steve took his dinner and hers into their bedroom.

From across the kitchen table Grandma said, "Wendy, eat your fish."

I pushed my fish around with a fork, made faces, and continued to eat only my mashed potatoes and corn niblets.

"It'll make you smart. It's brain food," she added.

"If the fish was so smart it wouldn't get caught," I answered. "Anyway, cauliflower is brain food. It's got left and right lobes and everything. See? I'm smart already. Smart enough not to eat this fish."

"Wendy." My father can sometimes say just one word—my name—in such a way that you don't want to hear him say anymore. That's how he said it, only he said more.

"The fish is delicious. Your grandmother worked

hard preparing this nice dinner for all of us. Just eat and keep your mouth shut."

"Now that"—I couldn't resist a good line—"is physically impossible."

Grandpa burst out laughing; Grandma gave him a look that could kill, and my mom changed the subject.

"I took a deposition in a lawyer's office today on this most interesting case," she said, "about a person who choked on a fishbone in the emergency room of a hospital while trying to give all the insurance information the admitting nurse insisted on getting."

Sometimes I think my mother makes up appropriate stories to change subjects and ease tensions. While Grandma and Daddy added their hospital admission aggravations, Grandpa and I switched plates so he got my fish, and I got his mashed potatoes and corn niblets.

But Mom's next words surprised me. She said she'd spoken to someone in the guidance department at my school about my detentions.

"Detentions?" Grandpa said. "History repeats itself, huh Douglas?" And he winked at my father, who looked like he wanted to say to my Grandpa Lou, "Just eat and keep your mouth shut," but couldn't talk back to his father.

"You had detentions, Dad?" I couldn't resist asking.

"Things were different then," Dad answered. "I was protecting my brother, the big shot, who'd pick a fight and tell everyone his brother, me, would take care of them."

Steve and Marissa stayed in their room, talked, and used the telephone all evening. I couldn't make out what was going on other than that. I felt a little sorry for Marissa. Everyone was telling her what to do. She's always seemed uncomfortable at big family get-togethers. I don't think she can handle crowds. We're all used to it. But, at least that night, thanks to Grandma and a little oatmeal, we all got a good night's sleep.

After breakfast the next morning, as I was leaving, Grandma stuffed this aluminum-foil square package into my pocketbook and muttered something like, "Lunch."

On the way to school Brenda told me she thinks Robby Marshall is in love with her. "How do you know?" I asked.

"He loaned me his notebook and he'd doodled my name all over the cover." Jennifer and I agreed immediately that meant in love or at least heavily in "like." I got this little mean feeling about how great it would have been if Brenda had borrowed his notebook and he'd doodled "Wendy" all over it.

"Is Gary silly to work with?" Brenda asked.

"No. He must be great to work with, unlike Sherman Barker," Jennifer answered for me. "Gary's grown up a lot over last summer. He's serious about things that matter, but he's still funny."

"I don't mind. Gary's okay," was all I said as I looked up the block to see if he was in sight.

Next, the unexpected happened. Gary, the only kid I know who has had five years of perfect attendance and always gets the perfect attendance award, was absent today. I was worried. It seemed odd to walk to school without him. We usually all walk together.

English was okay. We learned about adjectives and had to write the letters of our first names and find a perfect adjective with each letter to describe our personalities. I wrote "Witty Eager Nervous Devoted Youthful."

In health class, Mrs. Devin didn't have us read our baby log entries because we had a guest mother who actually demonstrated how to bathe a baby. You have to watch the baby every minute, and before you put the baby into the tub or bathinette, you have to test the water with your elbow to see it's not too hot. And you have to make sure not to let the baby slip out of your hands. The kids in the front row got drenched. The baby splashed so much she sent surfing waves over the sides of the plastic tub. We all laughed and I wished Gary was there. We could have made up a million bath jokes. I glanced toward the doorway a lot hoping he'd walk in, but he didn't.

Mrs. Devin reminded us that our baby logs would be collected tomorrow. "Since you have yourselves experienced childhood and are experiencing teenage years," she also said, "we will go on to study mid-life and old age during the second and third weeks of this life cycle project. Details to follow."

I telephoned Gary during lunch, from the phone booth outside the lunchroom. He answered the phone imitating an answering machine. "You have reached the Weiss residence," he said. "None of us are in the mood to talk right now, so at the sound of the tone leave your name, number, and a brief message. The Weiss of your choice will return your call later." Then he made a beeping tone followed by an operator voice that said, "Sorry your call did not go through. Hang up and dial again."

"Gary," I said, "I am not hanging up. I know you don't have an answering machine. What is going on there? Why aren't you in school? I'm really worried."

"Listen, Wendy," he said. "I can't talk now."

"Then I'm coming over after school to see for myself," I said.

"N.G. Also not possible."

"Why is it no good?" I pushed for an answer. "I'm not giving up. I know something's wrong. I can hear it in your voice. We're family now. You can trust me."

"Okay. Listen. Don't come over. Just meet me on the avenue at three-thirty in front of the fruit stand, and I'll try to make some sense out of all this."

"See you then," I said, just as the operator interrupted with the words, "Your time is up. Please deposit . . ."

"Bye," I said, and hung up before the sentence was completed.

Jennifer, Brenda, and Robby had saved me a seat at their table. "If Gary's not in school he must have appendicitis, pneumonia, and a broken leg," Robby said.

"No, he doesn't sound sick," I said. "I'm going to meet him on the avenue later and find out more."

Brenda and Robby were eating their pizza slices and at the same time were holding each other's hand. Jennifer looked on, starry-eyed. I just decided not to look at them.

I took out this squished aluminum-foil square that Grandma had stuffed into my pocketbook on my way out this morning. I could hardly wait to see what it was. I always buy school lunch, especially on pizza day like today. I peeled back the foil as the others watched.

"What is that?" Jennifer pointed to my black pumpernickel bread. I opened the slices and we determined by look, smell, and taste, that it was spread with a filling of cream cheese and crushed dates and nuts.

"This is something my grandma could have learned from only one person," I said. "My sister-in-law Marissa." There was a note under the sandwich. I read it out loud.

Dear Wendy,

Marissa mentioned to me yesterday, when she was still talking to me, that school lunches contain entirely too much salt, sugar, preservatives, and food coloring, and could be the cause of you getting hyper and into trouble so much. So try this. Maybe Marissa will be happy that I listened to her this time. Maybe she'll come out of her room.

Love,
Grandma

"Great," I said. "Grandma wants to make up with Marissa, and I get to suffer with pumpernickel bread." I was beginning to lose my patience. It's one thing to put up with everyone telling me what to do at home. That was tough enough. But now it was even creeping into my school lunch. What I eat for lunch is my very own business. Was I now losing even the little independence I'd had? I gave the sandwich to Sherman Barker, who will eat anything, and I bought a slice of pizza.

I got out of French class because I was called down to the guidance office. I wondered if my horoscope was right. We have this weird guidance counselor who has been known to tell kids she can't deal with them because their horoscope isn't right that day. She probably checks your birth date before sending for you. She wanted to know if I could explain the reason for my detention schedule.

I thought of Grandpa Lou winking at my father last night and saying, "Detentions? History repeats itself huh, Douglas?" "I've been told it's hereditary. I get it from my father," I said. "It's a medical thing from all the sugar and preservatives in school food."

"Oh," she said, but gave me a warning anyway.

Finally school was over. Jennifer and I walked home together after waiting in the fenced-in schoolyard around five minutes for Brenda, who never showed up. Some other kids told us she and Robby had left already.

"She could have at least told the other kids to tell us not to wait," I said. "She doesn't even think about us anymore. It's as if Robby has moved in and taken over her entire brain."

"Does she call you?" Jennifer asked. "She doesn't call me. And her line is always busy."

"No, she doesn't call me either, and I've given up trying to get through to her," I answered. "Do you think that always happens when a boy enters a girl's life?"

83.

"I think so," Jennifer said. "Because you haven't called me either since Gary entered yours."

Her words took me by surprise. Had a boy entered my life? Even now, as I walked with Jennifer, I knew my brain was thinking about meeting Gary on the avenue at three-thirty. Nah, I said to myself. It wasn't the same thing.

"A lot of people have entered my life," I explained to Jennifer. "They've not only entered, they've moved in. Have I mentioned to you the latest arrival of my grandfather?" But as we got to my corner I said, "I'll call you tonight."

I really didn't feel like getting into a conversation with anyone this afternoon. I unlocked the door, no longer checking to see if it was ajar or if any windows were open, no longer stopping to listen for unusual sounds. But I was still a latchkey kid at heart. I still wore my key on a string around my neck, hidden under my sweatshirt from possible molesters. And now I was wishing I was a latchkey kid once again. I put my books down on the table under the big mirror in the foyer, then called out loud and clear, "I'm home but I'm going out." I headed for the door, but not quickly enough. Suddenly there was an interrogation by grandparents in stereo. My grandfather's voice entered my left ear, traveling at high speed from the couch in the living room about six feet away. My grandmother's voice entered my right ear, growing closer and closer as she approached from the dining room saying the same words.

"Where are you going and when will you be back?"

Marissa was probably still in her room, not even coming out to see why Jory was crying.

"I'm going to the avenue to meet Gary at the fruit stand," I said. "I'll be back in an hour or so." I felt two years old. I was not used to explaining everything to everyone.

"A date with a boy?" Grandpa said.

"And you're not going to change out of that sweatshirt?" Grandma added, fingering my sleeve as if touching something she'd found in the garbage pail.

"I'm just meeting Gary on the avenue. And what's wrong with my sweatshirt? Sweatshirt is the fabric of the eighties. And speaking of dates, the only ones I've had were in my lunch today. That's what it was, dates, wasn't it?"

"Yes. Did you enjoy it? Did you stay out of trouble?" Grandma asked.

In order to get out I decided to say, "Yes, good-bye" and do an about-face and quick exit. As I raced down the steps, Grandma called after me.

"Pick up a head of lettuce, four tomatoes, and three bananas. Tell Al, the owner, it's for me—the one who moved to Florida but is back, so you won't get soft ones. Here's money." Grandma held out some crumpled bills she had in her pocket as I came back up the steps.

I took off before she could think of anything else. If I ran most of the way I'd make it to the fruit stand on Avenue J by three-thirty. And Gary had better be there. If he wasn't I'd go straight to his house and find out what was going on, once and for all.

9.

I JOGGED UP Seventh Street to Avenue J and made a right turn, glancing at Brenda's big corner house with the sign on its lawn that said BIL RAY—LET US PERMA-STONE YOUR HOUSE. I wondered if Robby was there with her. I continued past the candy store on the corner. When the light turned green I crossed Coney Island Avenue, zigzagging around the women pulling their grocery-bag-filled, two-wheel shopping carts behind them. I love the way the air smells on the avenue. First it's Chinese food smells dancing out of the Chinese restaurant, Joy Fong. Then it changes to barbecued chicken drifting in curly waves from the door of the kosher deli. I usually stop to look at the rotisserie turning the crisp, dripping, golden chicken, but today I forced my way onward. I passed the pizza place and bakery, and arrived at the fruit stand, which was piled high with pyramids of red apples next to hills of oranges and grapefruits, tomatoes, cucumbers, and lettuce.

Standing there munching on an apple was Gary. He waved and I waved back. My throat felt dry and my heart was pounding. I decided I better jog more. I haven't been alone in the house to dance and I'm getting out of shape.

"So what did I miss in school today?" Gary asked.

When I caught my breath I answered, "Why did you miss it is what I want to know."

When Gary said, "I'll get to that," I started to fill him in on the day.

I told him about the baby that was bathed in class and that Mrs. Devin was collecting the baby photos and logs tomorrow.

"She's collecting the babies?" he said. "What does she have, a photo gallery or the baby photo hall of fame?"

I was glad to see that no matter what had happened today, he could still joke.

"She has to grade them," I answered.

"Come on," he said, putting his hand on my shoulder and changing the subject. "Let's cross over and I'll buy you a cookie at Stern's."

"Okay, but you better start talking. What is going on in your house? You hang up your phone suddenly. There's a moan and a crash. It's really making me worried." We crossed the street, avoiding a guy on a delivery bike with its basket full of brown bags marked C & C BUTCHER.

"It's a long story," Gary said. "And I don't know when it began or where it's going to end. It's my grandmother. She's been acting really strange."

"I can relate to that, having several grandparents living with me. They sure are strange sometimes. Like my grandmother offers me cookies and says, 'Don't fill up on them. You'll spoil your dinner.'"

"Your grandparents are just being grandparents," Gary said. "That's not what I meant. Take last night

87.

when we were on the phone. I'd just turned away from Grandma for a second to call you. My parents were out and I'd been keeping an eye on her all evening as they said I should. In one second, she'd tried to take this pot from the stove and she touched the hot part and dropped it. She moaned and the pot crashed and I ran in to help her. I put her fingers in cold water and she moaned not in pain but as if she was just now remembering that pots can be hot. My grandmother is a very smart person. She's cooked for years. She even ran a restaurant herself after my grandfather died. If anyone knows pots are hot when there's a flame under them, it's her. But she kept saying, 'I forgot it was cold.' She kept saying cold instead of hot. I'm telling you. She scared me."

"Has that ever happened before?" I asked as we entered the bakery, breathed in the mouth-watering smell, and took a number from the machine. We stood next to each other in line.

"No. Not as bad as that," Gary said, answering my question. "She hasn't been herself for a while, though. She's always tired, and if I try to show her how to do something like turn up the thermostat, I have to show her over and over. She used to learn things if she was shown once. And she only wants to be with people she knows. That's why I can't invite friends over."

I had this big lump forming in my throat. Gary was being so serious. I wasn't used to it. I felt sad for him. I just reached out and took his wrist in my hand. My own family problems seemed so small compared to his. And he went on, "We can't leave my grandmother alone in the house, and both my parents work. We have this homemaker that comes in when I'm in school, but she has to leave by three o'clock when I get home. She's got kids to pick up at school. So I usually stay with Grandma till my mom gets home from the bank. It's not a big deal. She gets home by three-thirty or so. But today the homemaker's kid was sick and Mom had an important meeting and my dad was out of town on a business trip so I had to stay home. What I need now is a good cookie to take my mind off it."

"We're next," I said as we moved up to the tall, wood-and-glass, real old-fashioned counter. "Everything looks so good."

"My favorite's those curls of dough filled with chocolate and dipped in chocolate at each end," Gary said.

"I like them too," I agreed, even though the rectangle cookies of maple syrup and nuts are my favorite.

"Next," the lady in the white uniform said.

"We'll have four of these." Gary pointed to his favorite cookie.

After he paid we walked outside. It seemed kind of odd to be munching and enjoying these delicious cookies while we were talking about such a sad story. It felt to me like we were doing something bad. But Gary was enjoying his cookie and licking the melting chocolate off his fingers. It didn't bother him. "Don't you want your second cookie?" he asked.

"They're delicious, thanks," I said, "but why don't you eat this one?"

"Good," he said. And taking it from my hand he popped it all in his mouth at once. As he talked he looked like a squirrel with its cheeks full of acorns. "My mother said that when my dad gets back from his trip they'll take Grandma to the doctor again. Mom already called. She couldn't get an appointment till next week, anyway. But today, Grandma didn't seem so bad at all, except when she couldn't get the punch line of a joke I told her. She always tells jokes and gets punch lines. I get my sense of humor from her. Even worse was when she tried to follow me out when I left, but Mom got her."

"I'm sorry you're having trouble," was all I could think to say.

"Come on," Gary said. "I have to pick up a few things at the appetizing store near the train station. Grandma loves sour pickles and sweet red peppers. At her restaurant there always was a dish of them on every table."

"Don't let me forget I have to pick up lettuce, tomatoes, and bananas at the fruit stand," I said.

"This is fun to do our food shopping together and get away from the kids. Who's photo-sitting Askhim?" asked Gary.

"I still have him in my pocketbook."

"Never a moment alone." Gary laughed and took my hand and squeezed it. "My mom's taking care of Spot," he added as we approached Fifteenth Street.

I love the smell of the appetizing store, the pickles and smoked whitefish and lox. I love the window filled with different kinds of nuts and candies with apricots and marshmallow. I even love the way the man behind the counter puts pickled herring, chopped herring, farmer cheese, or cream cheese and lox spread into empty yogurt containers. The woman in front of us was arguing that lox is so expensive you have go to the Dime Savings Bank and take out a loan.

"But it's so good," the counterman said, adding, "you pay what you get for." Gary and I tried to hold in our laugh at the mixed-up words.

Gary made his selection and we headed for the fruit stand laughing, "You pay what you get for," instead of "You get what you pay for."

I bought the lettuce, tomatoes, and bananas with the owner Al approving them as worthy of "Mrs. Sokel, who moved to Florida but is back visiting."

"I'm used to working with older people, some who are forgetful," I confided to Gary. "I volunteer at the nursing home on Avenue K and Coney Island Avenue, sometimes." I don't usually talk about my volunteer work, but it's become so easy to talk to Gary that things just slip out. Gary didn't make a single wisecrack. He listened and I went on. "Sometimes I just talk to the people there and listen to their stories. Other times I make stuff like picture frames, and I bring the people gifts. Maybe I could make a picture frame for your grandmother, and you could tell her about me. Then I wouldn't be a stranger, and if you need help I could come over."

"Thanks," Gary said. "Now I think it's time to laugh again. Say something funny, okay?"

"I love mixed-up words. I collect them. My favorite was the time my mother yelled at me to 'Wipe off my buddy moots!'"

We both laughed. "I like them too," Gary said. "I've got a few favorites of my own. My aunt was

91.

changing my cousin's diaper and she said to me, 'You want to learn how to change a didy durper?'"

That one cracked me up. And Gary laughed when I told how in a restaurant my father had once ordered "whole-cornelled kern" instead of whole-kerneled corn. I liked making him laugh when I told him about Jory and how they're forming teams at my house, deciding whether Jory is really smiling or if it's gas. Mom, Dad, Marissa and Steve, and I say it's a real smile. Grandma and Grandpa say, "Nah, he's too young. It's gas." By the time we said good-bye at Tenth Street before I continued on to Seventh, we were both in better moods.

"Don't forget to bring Spot to school tomorrow and finish the baby log. Tomorrow it's on to teenage and early adult years," I called to Gary. "Life goes on."

He waved, and as he turned I saw this funny sticker on his rear jeans' pocket. It said, YOU'RE UGLY AND YOUR MOTHER DRESSES YOU FUNNY.

I jogged home—tripping occasionally over the sections of sidewalk raised by tree roots. The world seemed wonderful, and I had this joyful feeling of energy and a brain filled with Gary.

I came to a sudden halt in front of my house. Oh no. Something strange was going on again. Why was there a van in the driveway and two men in coveralls coming out the door looking like they'd just delivered something?

I was happy enough and stupid enough to dream that maybe it was my adopt-a-dog. I raced inside.

10.

I ZIGZAGGED PAST the taller of the two delivery people and read the lettering on the back of his gray coveralls: COMPUTRON INC. A computerized adopt-a-dog was definitely out, and the name, Computron Inc., rang a bell in my mind. That was the company Marissa used to work for as a programmer.

The door was still open and I walked inside. Marissa, Grandma, and Grandpa were standing in the living room staring at a computer. I actually saw Marissa hand Jory to Grandma and say, "Hold him a minute and I'll show you how this works." She sat down on a chair on wheels that had not been there when I left for school this morning, and patted the computer in front of her. She smiled and typed on the keyboard, "Hi Mac. It's good to see you again."

Wonder of wonders. Marissa smiling. She actually seemed to show an emotion called joy. I only saw her do that when Steve was accepted into med school and when Jory was a week old. She sure hasn't been smiling lately. Everything's been very serious to her. For a minute she even looked pretty. I thought she was going to introduce Mac to Jory as if it were his brother. I joined the group.

"Hi, Wendy." I read the green letters on the black screen. "Your mother left you an envelope taped on your bedroom mirror. This is Mac. He just moved in." Marissa typed this message on the keyboard in front of her.

I muttered something nasty like, "Always room for one more," kissed Grandma, Grandpa, and Jory hello, and headed for my room to see if Mom had any more surprises to notify me about.

I dumped my books on the desk and took the envelope from my mirror. In it was a note.

Wendy baby,

    Marissa has talked her company into letting her continue her job as programmer, at home. She doesn't want to leave Jory for the first few months. She said Dr. Pepper Feinback advises that the first six months to a year, the baby needs the parent, and of course Steve can't give up time from med school. Marissa has agreed to let Grandma help her as long as she's watching Grandma's every move. So now everyone will be happier, right? Even you? And maybe I'll get to work on time and not have to organize my own family court every morning. I'll have to work late tonight to make up for time missed. Maybe Marissa will teach you how to use the computer? Be good, and by the way, Grandma asked me to tell you not to forget to turn off the lights and your stereo when you're out of the room.

                                    Love,
                                    Mom

P.S. No need to worry about the laundry or dishwasher—Marissa and Grandma took care of that.

I think if my grandmother had a car she'd also have a bumper sticker that would say SAVE ELECTRICITY— YOU NEVER KNOW.

I tossed the note onto my bed and went back to the living room, which apparently was now turning into Marissa and Mac's office. Mac was sitting in my favorite corner where I like to curl up and watch *General* and eat Oreos. Marissa was talking a mile a minute. "See, Grandpa, this is the daisy-wheel printer and this is the modem that connects right to the phone and I have direct access to the office computer."

"Does that mean you'll be using the phone a lot?" I asked. Invasion of my phone would absolutely be the last straw. I remember an article I once read in *Teen* magazine on being assertive. Now it was time to assert myself.

"It's part of my job," Marissa answered, as if that was the most important thing in the world. "My company has ordered a special line, but the telephone company said they are backed up on installations and it will take a week or two. Did you know that there is more knowledge stored up in this computer than in a whole medical library? Medical programming is my specialty," she said proudly.

"Great," Grandpa said, "and if the electricity goes out—no more knowledge. That's progress?"

I could see the teams forming. It would now be me and Grandpa against Marissa and Mac. All Grandma said was, "More buttons. Everything's got buttons. Speaking of buttons reminds me of sewing. Look what I made for Jory."

"What did you make?" I asked. My grandma is very creative when it comes to sewing. She used to make all these neat outfits for my Barbie dolls.

"Jory's so little," Grandma went on, "you take a rubber band and a pocket and you've got a pair of shorts. I was just trying them on him when the Mac arrived. I better go put long pants on him so he doesn't get a chill. Shorts are for when he'll visit me in Florida." Grandma walked, kissing Jory's cheeks with each step. "Wendy, there's fresh fruit salad for your snack," she called after her.

"The shorts are adorable, Grandma," I said, walking partway with her.

I went into the kitchen, ignored the suggested snack, and took a glass of milk and a box of Oreos. I headed back to the living room, and Independence Lesson #2—Assert yourself. I turned on the TV loud and sat down at Marissa's feet to watch *General*.

"Wendy, what are you doing?" Marissa asked, not even looking up. "Shush," she added, and just went on pushing lettered key button after key button faster and faster. "Turn off the TV," she said. "I have to start working on a program. I have to have quiet to think."

"Speaking of programs," I said, "I'm watching *my* program and I'm eating pure sugar and chocolate. Grandpa, you want one?" I added, offering him the box.

"Now you're talking," he said, helping himself to a cookie.

"Wendy, turn down that TV set. I'm working," Marissa repeated. "It's important."

"Well this is my living room you're working in and I'm watching my favorite program," I answered. "It's important to me."

"How can you compare the importance of my work with your watching one hour of some silly soap?" Marissa said. "Turn it off."

"Stop bossing me," I said. "You're not my mother, you know. Some silly soap?" My voice raised an octave. "Laura is alive and has just returned to Luke but her life is in danger and . . ." I went on and on until I talked Marissa right out of the room. I mentally put a check mark next to Independence Lesson #2.

"Don't talk to Marissa that way," Grandma scolded me. Even Grandpa clicked his tongue.

"I'm sorry," I said. "I'm very mixed up and angry right now. And no one understands me . . . not even me." Then I hugged my grandma and the anger went away because I was glad she was healthy. As I thought of Gary's grandmother, my own problems shriveled back to the right size, like one raisin instead of a bunch of grapes.

97.

After *General* was over I took a shower and washed my hair, because for once there wasn't a lineup and the water would still be hot. Then I went directly to Independence Lesson #3 and announced to Grandma, "I'm going over to my friend Jennifer's house." Her reaction was just as I expected.

"You're going outside with a wet head? You'll catch a cold."

"I always go out with a wet head," I said. "I've been going out with a wet head for years. You've just never seen me do it. And in the past three years I've only had one cold so I don't think I'll get a cold today. Goodbye. I'll be back at six o'clock. If my mother, the ghostwriter, calls, tell her family court will still be in session later tonight. Better yet, I'll tape a note to her mirror."

"Why do you sound so angry?" Grandma asked.

"Me? Angry?" I said.

I was trying to unknot my sneaker lace as I spoke. Finally I resorted to using my teeth, only I forgot I had put my retainer in my mouth, and it got caught in the lace.

"You open your shoelace with two-thousand-dollar teeth?" Grandma said. That was the last I heard. I removed my retainer and tossed it and the sneaker it was attached to into my room. After putting on my old Adidas, I wrote the note, taped it to Mom's mirror, grabbed a jacket, and stormed out.

As I walked up Avenue K to Jennifer's house, I wondered if when I go off to college in five years I'll be able to get along with a roommate, and all those kids in a dorm, if I can't even get along with my grandmother and sister-in-law. Well, at least my sister Kerry would be calling tonight. She calls once a week to tell us how hard she's working and how rotten the food is at college. Tonight I really needed to talk to her. She'd understand how I felt.

It was nice and sunny out; kids were riding bikes and ringing their bells as they rode past me. Baby carriages were grouped around whichever house had a bench on its porch. Mothers sat comparing news of first teeth, first steps, first words, and toilet training while they yelled things like, "Jeremy, don't eat the pretzel if it dropped on the ground."

I walked into the apartment house where Jennifer lives and pushed the button next to her last name. She buzzed me in after I said my name into the intercom. The halls smelled like memories of meals passed, and tonight someone would definitely be eating liver and onions. Jennifer was waiting for me when the elevator opened at the third floor. She looked very happy to see me.

"I didn't know you were coming over," she said.

"Well, I was thinking about what you said about boys taking over girls' minds and all. Anyway, I decided to walk over. My house is not to be believed. Everyone and her computer has moved in. The invasion did not stop with Grandpa. Now we have Mac, Marissa's computer, making itself comfortable in my favorite spot in the living room, and using my phone so I can't even get calls. I'm too mad to even talk about it. What are you doing?"

"Nothing much. Just hanging around," she answered. "I was going to play some tapes. I got this new tape. It's awesome."

"Want to see if Brenda can come over too?" I asked.

"Sure," Jennifer said, "but I doubt if she will. Robby's probably over there finishing up their baby log to hand it in tomorrow."

My hand automatically went to my pocketbook where I'd placed the photo of Askhim for safe keeping. I had a strong desire to take it out and touch it, so that's what I did. It would seem strange not to have the twins anymore. I wondered if Gary would miss them, too. He might be too busy with the problems about his grandmother to even think about Askhim and Spot. I wondered if we'd see each other as much, or if he'd call me, once this part of the project was over.

Jennifer dialed Brenda's number but handed the phone to me. Brenda even has her own phone in her room with her own telephone number. "Hi," I said, "It's Wendy. I'm at Jennifer's. Want to come over and listen to her new Bruce Springsteen tape?"

"Oh, I have that one," Brenda said. "And anyway I can't, Robby's here. Wait till you see our baby book. It's the best. Say hi to Jennifer for me," she added, said good-bye, and hung up.

I delivered the message. "She says hi. She's busy with Robby finishing up their baby book."

"When Sherman Barker finished off our baby project on day two," Jennifer said, "you know what we had to do for the rest of the week?"

"What?" I asked. "I know you stayed after school once. And in health class I saw you take out this paper with numbers and names of magazines on it."

"We had to work with Mrs. Devin after school one

100.

day to research burial costs and stages of mourning like numbness, depression, anger, and recovery. It really grossed me out," Jennifer said as she pushed the button on her tape player and started moving to the beat of the music. "It inspired Sherman. He said he thinks now that he wants to be an undertaker when he grows up. As for the stages of grieving, I skipped numb and depressed and went directly to anger. I could have killed Sherman Barker for letting our baby photo go down that sewer."

"I'm sorry you lost your baby photo." I could feel her sadness.

I calmed Jennifer down and quickly put my baby photo back in my pocketbook.

Then Jennifer polished my nails and I polished hers this great purple color. And I looked through her earring collection and borrowed a pair to match my red sweater.

When I got home Grandpa took one look at me, turned to Grandma, and said, "See what happens? She goes out with a wet head—her nails turn purple." Then he messed up my hair and laughed. Grandma gave him and me one of her looks and the subject was dropped.

Daddy and Steve were home in time for dinner, which was Grandma's delicious veal parmigiana, and I realized I'd had no time alone with my father all week. The first thing I noticed was that his mustache was full-grown and he was trying to look dignified and used to it while eating mozzarella cheese. This was not easy. Then after dinner he announced he'd decided to start to jog and put on a sweatsuit he'd bought. Grandpa doesn't mess around. He took one look and cracked up laughing.

"Where'd you get the pajamas?" he teased, as if Daddy was a kid. Daddy did just what I would do. He pushed his chair back, as noisily as possible, and slammed the door on his way out.

I decided to jog after him and caught up half a block away. We ran together silently, but it felt so good, just us and the quiet starlit night. We were both winded by Tenth Street.

"I don't know how I got so out of shape overnight," Dad said.

"What about me? I'm not old enough to be out of shape. I haven't even gotten my shape yet."

We decided to toast the start of our physical fitness plan by walking to the luncheonette on Avenue J and Coney Island Avenue and having an egg cream. As we sipped we talked.

"I thought your mother and I were getting to a point where we'd have time alone," he said. "It's getting to be standing room only in our house. With Grandpa here, I don't even feel like an adult, and I'm forty-seven years old."

"Tell me about it," I moaned. "I understand what you mean, but you're hardly home. What about me? I suddenly have a litter of caretakers and order givers instead of the dog I wanted. It's really funny. You said I couldn't adopt a dog because you and Mom didn't want added responsibilities now that us kids were leaving the nest. You didn't want to be tied down with a dog after I go off to college in five years."

"That's still true, Wendy," Dad said. "The rest of

the invasion is only temporary. A dog is a long-term commitment."

"But it doesn't talk back and it doesn't boss you around," I answered, taking a last sip and wiping off my own chocolate mustache as my dad wiped at his real one, stroking it as if to be sure it was still there. Maybe he liked his mustache even more since Grandma had asked him, "What's with the eyebrow over your lip?"

We got home in time for Kerry's telephone call. She was all excited. "Four o'clock in the morning we had to evacuate the dorm because of a small fire in the hall garbage pail. It burned up through the ceiling. People pounded on the doors. It was funny to see who slept in pajamas and who didn't," she added, and giggled. It's a coed dorm.

"Did the girls blow-dry their hair before running out, or did they let the guys see them frizzy and all?" I asked, half teasing and half serious—not knowing for sure if Kerry was being dramatic. Kerry can make you believe anything. When I was little she had me believing that if you swallow a watermelon pit, a watermelon will grow in your stomach. She'd prove it to me by pointing out pregnant women.

Dad called to me, "Tell Kerry we know she calls on MCI, but MCI is thirty-five percent cheaper, not free."

Anyway, the result of the conversation was that Kerry would be home for the weekend, till her dorm room aired out, and so she could wash all her sweaters because they smelled like smoke.

"Boy, I can sure use a weekend away from a crowded dorm," she said.

"Then don't come home," I advised, not having time to talk to her as I'd planned. "It'll be like trading a headache for an upset stomach."

I spent the evening looking through the baby books Mom had kept on Steve, Alan, and Kerry. Steve's had photos, inoculation dates, trips taken, gifts received, first steps, words, and teeth all filled in and detailed. Alan's was pretty complete. Kerry's was almost complete, but not detailed. And mine had my name, my hospital photo, and a lot of blank pages. I finished my baby log, even adding a make-believe hospital identification bracelet. Gary didn't phone and I hoped nothing was wrong at his house. I didn't want to call him and interrupt anything.

Mom got home at ten-thirty, and Grandma practically fed her and put her to bed. Mom didn't seem to mind the attention one bit.

I crept into bed with her while my dad was watching the evening news. "Ma," I said, "let me introduce myself. I'm Wendy. It's been nice corresponding with you, but I want more than a pen pal. Tonight I want my mommy."

She hugged me close, like she'd just been hugged by her own mother. "You're having a hard time, aren't you, baby? I do understand that. Things aren't exactly like Daddy and I planned them either. I keep hoping everyone will be happy and adjust. I can't complain. It's a help to me, actually. Meals are cooked and served and I don't have to worry about you being home alone. Your father is enjoying having the baby around and is getting more used to the idea of being a grandfather, which to him had meant growing old. Haven't you noticed how your father has needed more of my attention? I feel guilty leaving you home and going out with him for dinner, but I know when he's the grumpiest and least lovable is really when he's working things through in his life. That's when he needs my love and attention the most."

I liked the feeling of my mom confiding in me about her private life. It made me feel older. Isn't it funny, I thought, I'm busy wanting to feel older and on my own, and Dad is trying to feel younger and wants more attention. It made me think about my parents being grandparents. Mom doesn't look like a grandma. Grandma Minnie looks like a grandma. Mom looks too young. But Grandma Minnie doesn't look old enough to be a great-grandmother, either. It's all very confusing for everybody.

I snuggled even closer to my mother. I took her hand and kissed it. "I'm sorry you're having a hard time, too," I said. Then she encouraged me to tell my feelings. Maybe Mom felt like she shouldn't complain, but I felt as if I should. "Take this deposition." I used one of her words to make her smile. "I can complain and I will. Sure I like special breakfasts served to me, but I have no privacy. I have to share my room. Everyone tells me what I can and can't do and what I should and shouldn't eat, and what I shouldn't watch on TV, and where and when I shouldn't watch it. I've got a nephew I have to sneak around to touch and a computer named Mac moved into my comfortable corner in the living room. I'm about to have a crisis moment."

"I'll give it a lot of thought." Mom yawned as she answered, apologizing for the yawn. "But you can't just expect people to be here to serve you breakfast and not be here at three o'clock.'' She sighed, then added, ''I just don't know what to do. Daddy and I haven't given up our room, but we've lost our privacy too, and I don't want serious problems to arise. I'm doing a lot of juggling here, and I feel like I'm about to drop something on my foot.''

I didn't quite understand what she meant. ''I'll give that a lot of thought, too,'' I promised, then kissed her good-night. As I was walking out of her room I said, ''Oh, did you hear? Kerry had a fire in her dorm and she and all her sweaters are coming home for the weekend. She's okay. No one was hurt or anything. I'm glad she's bringing her sweaters back, I've missed them.'' I think Mom was putting her pillow over her head as I walked out.

11.

IT WAS NOT easy to part with the baby photos the next day. Not for some of us, anyway. I mean, there were several kids who couldn't have cared less about the project, but for Gary and me it was a sad moment. Of course we tried to be funny but it didn't really come off.

I guess Mrs. Devin was prepared for our reactions, because after she collected the photos and our baby logs she said, "You can have fifteen minutes to talk privately with your partner—to discuss and write briefly about the advantages and disadvantages of parenthood." The class scattered to different corners of the room, and it was really special because Gary sat very close to me while we talked baby memories, and when time was up he even hugged me before going back to his seat. Out of the corner of my eye I saw Robby Marshall just wave to Brenda and walk over to this really pretty girl, Lisa.

It's still hard to believe that to raise a baby from birth to age eighteen costs $150,000 for food, clothing, education, and medical expenses. And costs a quarter of a million dollars if you add on a good college and grad school. We'd only needed to figure costs of the first year, but Gary and I wanted an A, so we did some extra research and figuring.

Mrs. Devin had some of us read out loud from our summary of disadvantages and advantages to having a baby. "You always have to remember to do things for more than yourself," Robby read.

"It was hard to go places with the pressures of feeding times," Brenda added. "And the baby's waking times were unbearable sometimes."

"It's not easy to get a sitter," Beverly Arnold called out.

"You're always cleaning up a mess and they cry for no reason," I said, then switched to advantages. "But the best part about having a baby is a couple being ready for it and wanting to take care of it together."

Then Gary continued reading the paragraph we'd written. "But we don't want to have the responsibility until we're married and know each other and can afford it. And we'd rather not live with our parents."

Next Mrs. Devin introduced the second week of the project. "Since you are teenagers, most of you have parents approaching or already in mid-life. I want you to observe, take notes, and write about the following: one, list five of your concerns as teenagers; two, list five of your parents' concerns in mid-life; three, list five things your parents frequently tell you; and finally, write a composition about something that signifies a parent's entrance into mid-life or mid-life crisis."

"Do we keep the same partners?" Brenda asked.

Mrs. Devin didn't hear Brenda's low voice, lost in the chatter of kids' reactions. She went on. "I'm also going to tell you the last part of this life cycle project

108.

now, even though it won't be due for two weeks. It explores the joys and problems of the elderly. I want you to notice your parents' relationships with their parents, write three descriptions of different people over age seventy, with various lifestyles, and I want you to visit the nursing home on Coney Island Avenue."

"Do we keep the same partners?" This time Brenda spoke up loud and clear.

"The final summary for the project is to describe the life cycle in your own way." Mrs. Devin finished her thought, then answered as she handed out dittos with all this information. "You won't need partners for this week's or next week's project."

About half the class cheered at that information, and the other half groaned with disappointment at the sound of so much work.

"Any questions?" Mrs. Devin asked.

Sherman Barker called out, "Does spelling count?"

The part of the assignment about visiting a nursing home made me decide to decorate more picture frame presents. Those people there that I'd already given frames to were pleased to get a present. I decided I'd make one extra for Gary's grandmother like I'd suggested to him. Then I'd have a good excuse to visit him and deliver it. When I looked at Gary, he was looking at me. I wondered if he would call me. I found myself hoping he would. He winked at me and I smiled back.

"I wonder if Robby will still call Brenda now that the paired part of the project is over," Jennifer said to me. "He seems to be paying a lot of attention to Lisa."

"I noticed," I answered. "Brenda may need us

again." Then I leaned toward Gary and asked, "How are things going with your grandma?"

"Don't ask," was his answer. So I didn't ask anything else. He didn't say a word about getting together after school or calling me.

The bell rang. Mrs. Devin sent us off with some pamphlets and the line, "Now onto mid-life—and beyond. Read, observe, and report. Good luck."

Only a few kids charged out of the room today. Most of us kind of lingered and inched our way out.

Later in the day, on the way home from school, Brenda walked with us. Robby was still talking to Lisa when we left. "Go on ahead," he'd called.

"I don't know why we couldn't have kept our same partners for the second part of the project," Brenda said.

"I was thinking that too," I agreed honestly—not just to console her.

"Don't look at me," Jennifer said. "Two seconds with Sherman Barker was quite enough. So you like Gary, huh Wendy?"

"What's not to like?" was all I answered, but I knew there was much more to say only I didn't feel like telling anyone how I felt yet. I just wanted to feel it, a kind of inside happy feeling that makes you smile or laugh even when no one has said anything funny. I wasn't sure when I started to feel it, but I think it was when we were walking home from the avenue yesterday.

Back at my house, Kerry and her sweaters had already arrived. She'd gotten a ride home from college with a friend. Every sink and even the bathtub was filled with soaking sweaters. The washing machine was going, and I found Grandma and Kerry folding laundry from the dryer. Kerry smelled like a fire sale when I hugged her. We even kissed each other. We only did that on birthdays before she went away to school.

I had so much I wanted to talk to her about—alone. But there was no such thing as alone in this house. Grandma gave me the snack menu of peanut butter and whole-wheat crackers, then a kiss hello, and went to turn the chicken. It looked like the only place to be alone with Kerry was in the laundry room right now.

"Oh, Alan's coming home tonight," Kerry informed me. "I called our long lost, non-writing brother. When he heard everyone was home eating real food, especially Grandma's specialties, he said he was on his way. So I'm squeezing in with you and Grandma tonight, and Alan will bunk with Grandpa."

"Do Mom and Dad know?" I asked numbly while counting on my fingers how many people would now be waiting for the bathroom.

"Negative," Kerry said. "It's so good to be home," she went on excitedly, "private bathrooms, with showers that you don't have to jump out of every time anyone announces, 'flushing,' or risk getting scorched, kitchen smells of roasting chicken, my family to hug me, no tests. Don't get me wrong, Wen, college is great, but coming home is special, and I've never done that before. You don't know how lucky you are."

"Lucky? Me?" I didn't really understand, but I knew it was a special moment for Kerry, because she even hugged and kissed me for no reason at all and neither one of us said, "Yuck."

"You're really independent now? Huh, Kerry?" I

111.

asked. "You stay up as late as you want and eat whatever you please."

"I stay up very late, studying," Kerry said, "and I live on Domino's Pizza."

"I'm trying to get ready to be independent," I explained. "But it's not easy around here." I folded a sweatshirt as I spoke. "How did you know when you were independent?" I asked her.

"That's easy," she said. "I knew I was independent when I couldn't scream, 'Daddy there's a spider in my room,' when I had to handle the situation myself."

"Yuck," I said. "Gross. I'll never be able to do that. If I see a fly I try to lead it out an open door or window. If I see even a spiderweb I call Daddy." The last mountain of clothes was folded when I said, "Want to watch *General Hospital* with me?"

"Sure," Kerry said. "TV, what a luxury. I've almost forgotten about it. Oh, and when does the baby get up from his nap? I can't wait to get my hands on that Jory."

"Marissa is not crazy about hands on Jory unless they're hers, Steve's, or, if she's watching, Grandma is allowed."

"You're kidding!"

"I wish," I said as we walked into the living room.

Marissa was seated at her computer, and Grandpa was standing and looking over her shoulder. She was showing him how to enter a message, and he was muttering things like, "Modem schmodem."

I walked over, said, "May I?" and typed in, "Hello Mac."

"Very good," Marissa said, and smiled at me until

she read the rest of my message: "Good-bye Mac. It's time for *General*."

"Put on the what-do-you-call-it opera," Grandpa said. "I'm very worried already about Luke and what's-her-name. So where are the Oreos?" he added.

I think I caught Marissa glancing at *General Hospital* today, but when she saw me look at her she got busy with her computer.

The telephone rang and I raced to get it. Gary usually called around this time. Today it was my father's secretary with a message that both my parents would be a little late getting home tonight. I wondered why.

I was disappointed that it wasn't Gary calling. Maybe that was it for us. No baby project, no romance. That thought worried me.

The TV ad for adopt-a-dog came on and I ran in to see it. Today's dog was a really special one. It was a hard-to-place handicapped older dog with one eye, a blond cocker spaniel. I absolutely fell in love with it. That gorgeous white, part poodle they'd shown yesterday now had the words *adopted* across its picture, as did the shaggy dog from earlier in the week. I'd hoped one of them would be mine, but no luck. My parents weren't ever around enough for me to convince them to let me adopt a dog.

I was getting annoyed at my folks. It wasn't fair that they didn't spend time home so they'd see how my life has changed. Lately they just seemed concerned with themselves and having fun.

We were all startled by pounding on the door. "Who's at the door, Mr. T?" Grandpa asked. "Keep your shirt on," he hollered as I went to open it.

113.

My brother Alan burst in behind two big duffle bags that smelled like the school gym after a basketball game. He dropped the bags, lifted me off the ground, and swung me around, a habit my brothers have had since I was little. I felt something funny against my face. I almost screamed when I got a good look at him. "You look like a bear," I said.

Alan stroked his newly grown beard and turned to show me his long hair.

Grandpa took one look at him, kissed him, and said, "There was a sale on hair at your college? This is what they teach there—to grow hair and beards?"

"That looks super," Kerry said. "Did you get your ear pierced, too?"

"No," Alan said, "I can't stand the thought of pain. Hey, Marissa, how's the world treating you?" Alan hugged and kissed Marissa who stiffened as the beard brushed by her.

"Really, Alan. Don't you think it's time to stop rebelling?" Marissa said.

"He's sowing his wild oats," Grandpa said. "If he can't sow them at twenty, when then? He'll grow a mustache when he's middle-aged and run around the streets in pajamas. I should have let your father keep his mustache when he was twenty." My father had a mustache at twenty? I never knew that, I thought.

"Who's sewing what?" Grandma came in. "Who are you? The Fuller Brush man?" She reached up to kiss Alan but could only get to his neck. "This is like kissing my fur coat," she said. Then she saw the duffle bags. "More laundry? Oy. There's no end to it. What's the matter, there are no washing machines at school?"

"And no barbers?" Marissa added.

Tonight, for once, I thought to myself, there'd be a few surprises waiting for Mom and Dad when they got home. Would Dad twirl his mustache while talking to Alan, who would be stroking his beard? That thought and Grandpa's mention of middle age gave me a great idea for my mid-life project. I definitely knew what the composition title would be. My assignment #4, to write a composition about something that signifies mid-life or mid-life crisis, would be called "Your Father's Mustache."

12.

I NEVER DID get to make the picture frame to give to Gary's grandmother. This turned into a strange evening. It was extra unusual for Mom and Dad to be late coming home on Friday night. We always have Friday night dinner together—it's tradition. Alan and Kerry didn't eat dinner, they attacked it. "Neanderthals!" Steve said. "This is a fork and this is a knife." He held up one of each.

"Grandma, this chicken and soup is the best," Kerry said, and Alan nodded in agreement, his mouth too full to speak. Grandma beamed happily, obviously enjoying the praise.

"It's all right, a little greasy but not bad," Grandpa just had to tease.

"Where is there grease?" Grandma defended herself, and the battle was on.

Grandpa asked about what courses Alan was taking in college. "I'm taking Rocks for Jocks," Alan answered. "It's the easiest science course. Geology for athletes."

Then Marissa started chattering about her job. "I'm categorizing diseases and correlating them with genetic and environmental information," she explained, "and with the age range affected. Mac is a storehouse of information. There's nothing he can't find if he's been programmed with enough data. I'm convinced of it."

"Can he find his way out of the living room?" I asked. Then looked down at my plate to avoid the look I knew I'd get.

"I had to go to the morgue today," Steve announced. "I knocked on the door before I went in." He laughed. "If anyone answered I think I would have jumped out of my skin."

"Do we have to talk about corpses and morgues at dinner?" Kerry asked.

"Chill out, Kerry," Alan said to calm her down. Steve changed the subject. He described open-heart surgery instead.

Marissa joined in, with the genetic and environmental causes of heart disease and the age most affected, and was going on and on when Jory started crying. Steve was giving information on medications used as alternatives to heart surgery, and Marissa was trying to remember if he'd named them all.

We all stopped eating mid-chew as Marissa said, "Could someone get Jory for me?" and went with Steve to check their answers with Mac.

I've noticed a change in her since the moment that computer of hers moved in. *She* is less like a computer and more human each hour.

This was my big moment. "I'll get Jory," I said as I took off for his room. I waited for Marissa to turn around and stop me but she didn't.

How do babies know when you're in the middle of dinner? It's as if they have radar. I lifted Jory out of the

117.

crib. He was sobbing and the back of his head was soaked with perspiration. That wasn't the only end that was soaked.

He looked up at me from the changing table as I laid him down.

"What a good boy," I said, in this silly little voice I never used before. As I spoke, Jory waved his arms and kicked his feet. I powdered him, changed his diaper, and dressed him in a fresh undershirt and stretch outfit. Then I carried him into the dining room kissing his fuzzy head all the way. From the adjoining room, Marissa looked at me. I thought she was going to say something about germs and the baby hasn't had his shots yet. I was surprised to see she had almost a sweet expression on her face. "Marissa, this is the cutest baby in the world," I said, and kissed Jory three more times.

Grandma looked at me and Jory, and said, "You are the two cutest babies in the world." That made me feel good enough to even think nice things about Marissa, things like how we both love Steve and Jory. But I wasn't ready to say anything more yet.

We passed Jory around the table. He wasn't much bigger than the plate of chicken we'd passed around a while earlier. He was happy as could be. We all laughed if he hiccuped or burped, as if he was the greatest show on earth. I looked around the table at my family and felt like I was in the middle of a beautiful family photo. Only Mom and Dad were missing, and the photo turned into one of those "what's wrong with this picture?" puzzles. Maybe something *was* wrong. They don't usually have secretaries phone for them and give messages, and they always insist on knowing where I am and always tell me where they are.

The telephone rang. I felt split in half. Half of me hoped it was Gary and the other half hoped it was Mom or Dad. Both halves hoped it would be a good call, but it wasn't.

Gary was on the phone and he sounded awful. "It's all my fault," he said.

"What is it?" I asked, nervously twisting the phone wire.

My family got very quiet, and I could see they were listening and looking at me anxiously. I guess we were all worried about Mom and Dad.

"I had an argument with my mother about having to spend this coming Sunday watching my grandmother," Gary explained. "I know my father will be back tonight and they have a wedding to go to on Sunday, but I had planned something special for Sunday afternoon."

What did that mean? I wondered. And did it involve me? I wished it did.

"Anyway, I wasn't thinking. When I went to take the garbage out," Gary continued, "I left the door open and . . ." He stopped to swallow hard. I could even hear him swallow. "My grandmother must have walked out behind me and gone around the back of the house when I went to the street in front to where the pails are. We can't find her anywhere."

"You lost your grandmother?" I said.

Grandpa asked, "Who are you talking to? Who died?"

"Can I help you look for her?" I offered. "We have

so many people in my house. We could form an instant search party."

"What is she talking about?" Grandma said. "Wendy, who is that?"

"It's for me. It's Gary," I said, "and he's got trouble at his house."

"A few of my parents' friends are organizing into a search group, but my parents don't have many friends anymore. Some have moved and others have dropped them because they've been so tied down with my grandmother," Gary said. "I called to hear your voice, and besides, you always have good ideas. It would be great if you and your family would help. We've got to comb the neighborhood. My mother called the police, and they upset her when they said you have to wait at least twenty-four hours for a missing person. That's ridiculous."

"I'm sure we can all help," I said, and I really did feel sure, even without asking, that my family would help me in my friend's emergency. I liked that feeling. "Come over and we'll organize and get going."

I explained the situation to the rest of the group.

"Of course we'll help." Grandpa spoke first but everyone agreed.

Marissa and I made plans. "For a start, we'll need a photo, a description, a list of her symptoms, too," she said, "because I plan to use Mac and see if he can help us."

"And a list of places she usually likes to go to," I added. "Now if I had a dog, it could smell a piece of Gary's grandmother's nightgown and find her like on

TV, and while it was out maybe it could find Mom and Dad too."

"You sure want that dog, don't you?" Marissa said.

"No kidding," I answered sarcastically.

"I'm really getting worried about your parents," Grandma put in. "Where do you suppose they are?"

"I don't know," I said. I don't like the way it feels to wait and wait when you don't know where someone you love is. For the first time I realized that's probably why Mom always called to see if I was home from school in my latchkey-kid days. Maybe it wasn't because she was treating me like a baby. Maybe if she didn't call she'd have this awful wavy feeling in her stomach like I had.

Jory fell asleep in Grandma's arms, and Steve took him back to the crib. A baby's life looks so peaceful and easy, but maybe it isn't to a baby. Maybe my life looks easy to my parents.

The doorbell rang, interrupting my thoughts. I hoped it was Mom and Dad, even though I knew it probably was Gary.

"Hi," he said, exhaling and catching his breath. He must have raced over. "Here." He handed me a photo and talked in one-word sentences till he could breathe regularly again. "My mother's staying in the house in case the police call back. She got them to start looking for Grandma by telling them she needs to take her medicine. My dad's due back from his business trip anytime now."

I showed the photo of his grandmother to the rest of my family, thinking that the woman in the photo looked familiar to me. "I think I once saw her visiting at the nursing home while I was volunteering there."

"What a beautiful woman," Grandpa said. "She has talking eyes."

"Didn't she run that restaurant on Ocean Avenue?" Grandma said, studying the picture. "When my Sammy was alive we ate there many times." She seemed to enjoy the memory—even taste it. "You know, I sometimes think about opening a restaurant in Florida. I've always loved to cook, and what's missing there is home cooking—that's what I'd name the restaurant, 'Minnie's Home Cooking.'"

Next we all gathered around Mac, the computer. Marissa and I asked Gary a lot of questions.

"Her name is Frieda Weiss," Gary answered, "and she's five feet tall and weighs about one hundred five pounds. She has blue-gray hair and a mole on her chin. Her eyes are brown."

"I'm going to check the hospitals," Steve announced. "Just to see if she wandered in or if anyone found her and brought her there—or if she's been in an accident."

"Maybe you should check and see if Mom and Dad were in an accident, too," I said, only half seriously. What really got me scared was that Steve answered, "I planned to do just that."

I guess whenever I'm scared I joke. It gets me by the bad moment. Gary, too. "It's ten o'clock." I started quoting a TV commercial message about knowing where your children are. "Do you know where your parents are?" And Gary substituted "grandmother" at the instant I said "parents." But we only laughed for a second or so.

Marissa entered the data into Mac—symptoms, prescribed medications, and age. "I don't have to go on line to my office computer for this, so the phone won't be tied up," she explained.

Gary dictated, and I made a list of all the places Frieda Weiss loved, traveled to, lived, or worked. I also listed friends and relatives she visited, temples she attended, and a million other things. Then we divided up the neighborhood and set up pairs. Marissa was paired with Mac. She was entering all this information and storing it in Mac's memory bank. She would be home to work on him and watch Jory.

"You can't go," Grandma said to Grandpa. "You're recuperating from injuries."

"There's nothing wrong with my legs or my eyes and ears," he answered. "I don't use my wrist and shoulder to see and find someone. Don't hock me, Minnie. I'm getting *spilkas*, splinters in my behind, from sitting around doing nothing. I'm used to activity and excitement and hard work—and romance!" Grandpa added.

"I'll go with you, but if you get tired we'll come right back," she agreed.

Of course I was paired with Gary, and we were given the immediate area. We decided on a meeting time, then Steve and Alan set off in Steve's car. Kerry was paired with the telephone and got busy phoning all the numbers Gary's mother had suggested he bring from Mrs. Weiss's address-and-phone-number book. She'd also sent a note thanking us for our help.

I put on my jacket and went outside with Gary. It was a dark night, just a sliver of moon and freckles of stars. Some of the night sounds on Brooklyn side streets are different from the day sounds. Sirens are the same and car horns are the same. But at night, in the quiet of the dark you hear only a few hurried footsteps instead of lots of feet and voices. And you hear cats clawing at the garbage pails, sometimes sending the lids crashing, or you hear cats partying or fighting. Occasionally a door slams or a baby cries, but most of the time there is an eerie stillness, a loneliness if you're by yourself, and a closeness if you're with someone. Gary and I felt that closeness tonight. We held hands as we walked, and it momentarily soothed our fears and worries about his grandmother and my parents—enough to let us concentrate on trying to find Frieda Weiss. I don't know if holding hands in times of trouble counts as romance, but it felt very nice.

Every few minutes Gary would call out, "Grandma, do you hear me?" as we'd come to an alley. But the only answer we got was from the super of a building on Ocean Parkway who said, "I hear you kids—now beat it."

I'm not a time person. Sometimes an hour seems like a minute to me, and other times it seems like a day. I don't even have a digital watch. Gary was the time-keeper. We were all to meet back at my house or phone back in three-quarters of an hour to compare notes and plan our next strategy. I hoped Mom and Dad would be home when we returned.

I tried to think why they'd be so late. I told Gary my worries and he squeezed my hand. I remembered some things they'd said last evening. When I was having an egg cream with Dad, he'd talked about not having time alone with Mom anymore. And when I talked to Mom last night after she was in bed, she talked about having too much to juggle or something like that. I guess things have been pretty tough for them, too. Maybe I'm not the only one who finds living in this house a pain right now. I'd heard of runaway teenagers, and places that help them, like hot lines to call. I've heard of runaway fathers deserting the family, or of runaway mothers. But I'd never heard of a home or hot line for runaway parents.

Then again, maybe they were mugged. That's a fact of life in the city. My grandfather has this solution to it, "Speak softly and walk a big dog." Hey, that was an angle I hadn't tried yet, safety in the streets when I'm alone—a good reason to adopt a dog. I'd been pestering for a small, compact, easy-care dog. Wrong approach. I should have talked about big and protective—a city dog. But then again, who's alone anymore?

We returned home, unsuccessful. Grandma and Grandpa were already home. Grandma made a pot of decaffeinated coffee. "You'll drink something warm. It will calm you and you think better," she explained. I remembered when my Grandpa Sam died three years ago, someone was always making coffee.

"We didn't go very far," Grandma said. "Big shot over here"—she pointed to Grandpa Lou—"he thinks he's strong as an ox. I say he's stubborn as a mule. Injuries take your strength away for a bit."

"All I had to do was sigh and yawn, and she dragged me home," Grandpa interrupted. "Talk about strong

125.

as an ox, she's it. She's got hands with the power of an arm wrestler, your grandmother."

"That's because I always open up my own jars," she answered proudly. Grandma seemed happy to have someone to watch over and order around, I observed.

I could see Gary was getting very anxious again. He sat at the kitchen table, but his whole body was moving—toes tapping, fingers strumming on the butcher-block tabletop, body twisting on the swivel chairs.

"Did Steve call?" I asked.

"Yes," Grandma said. "He and Alan are on their way back. He said there's nothing on record in the hospitals." That was good news in a way, but not knowing where someone was felt worse than finding out someone was in the hospital.

"Where's Kerry?" I asked.

"Did she have any leads with those phone calls?" Gary added.

"No," Grandpa said. "It's sad, but most of the people in Mrs. Weiss's address book had died, were in the hospital or nursing home, or had moved to Florida. She tried to call the friends at the nursing home, but it was too late for calls to be put through. Kerry wanted to do something to help. So she called the TV station, and if we bring a photograph over they'll show it on the late late news. We've already missed the deadline for the eleven o'clock news. She's waiting for Steve and Alan to drive her over."

I could see a warm drink was not going to help Gary. What he needed was the same thing I needed: action. "Any word from Mom and Dad?" I asked.

"They're gonna get it from me when they get home," Grandpa said.

It sounded like Mom and Dad were teenagers. And that was one of the lines my parents say to me a lot when they call from the office and I give them a hard time about wanting to go to Coney Island or someplace with my friends. I always wondered what "it" is. Maybe Grandpa knew.

"Do you think we should call the police?" I suggested.

"We'll give them till midnight," Grandma said. "They did have that secretary call, after all."

"But the message was they'd be a little late," I reminded her. "Come on, Gary, let's check with Marissa and the computer."

"I better call my mom first, before it gets any later," he said. We went into the living room. He phoned, and then gave me an update. "My dad got home and he's already brought a photo to the TV station in time for the news. All we can do now is wait."

"Let's check the computer. So is Mac another Sherlock Holmes, or what?" I asked.

"Well," Marissa answered, "I'm afraid he's just a computer and can only do what he's programmed for. He can't find your grandmother, Gary, but he has come up with a number of very interesting facts about her. He's suggested what her problem might be, and that's a help."

"Like what?" Gary asked.

Just then we were interrupted by what you might call one of the more ridiculous scenes I've ever observed. My mom and dad practically burst through the front doorway in a full-fledged giggling fit. I'm talking belly laughs and collapsing and leaning on each other kind of laughter, with some choking and gasping. I could have died of embarrassment with Gary seeing all this except I was so relieved to see them alive, well, and unmugged. At this moment especially, in fact all evening, I'd felt glad to have so many people around who love me and who I love.

As for Mom and Dad, there was no smell of alcohol or anything weird. They're not into that kind of stuff. But they seemed to be drunk on laughter just after they'd come in. We couldn't even get their attention to tell them a tragedy was going on. In this crowd, they didn't realize that a non–family member, an unknown kid, Gary, was in the room.

The only thing that stopped them was when Steve and Alan returned. They stared in surprise and shock to see Alan home, with a beard and long hair. Their mouths dropped open. Alan pointed to Dad's mustache. It seemed like almost everyone in my house had a lot of explaining to do.

13.

WE WERE ALL crowded around partly in the foyer and partly in the living room. Mom and Dad glared at Alan's long hair and beard. They started to give "it" to Alan. Grandpa, however, was ready to give "it" to them.

"Where have you been?" he roared, and Mom and Dad stopped talking and stared at him. "What is the meaning of worrying everybody sick and then walking in here as if it's a big joke?" Grandpa asked Mom and Dad in the same tone of voice that I've heard them use with Steve, Alan, Kerry, and me. "It's Friday night. You should have been home for dinner with your family. You two are acting like rebellious teenagers!"

"What are you talking about? It's before midnight." Dad defended himself like one of us kids.

"Do you remember when you two were dating, and missed the last train home from a party on Long Island?" Grandpa said, and looked at my father. "Your mother and I were frantic. You promised never to worry us like that again!"

It was really neat to hear my parents treated like kids and to hear about how they'd sometimes gotten into trouble, too. I looked at Kerry and Alan and smiled.

"Pop," Dad said, "now hold everything. Didn't you get a phone call from my secretary? I did learn from that teenage mistake," he admitted, and looked at Alan, Kerry, and me, and even at Steve. "You taught me then to phone if I was going to be late. It's the considerate thing to do. I have always called so you wouldn't worry." At this moment, even Mom and Dad didn't seem all that independent.

"Susan," Grandma now started in on Mom, "that secretary told us you would be a little late. That means an hour to me, no more. You don't know what has been going on around here."

"She was not supposed to say a little late," Dad said. "I told her to say before midnight."

"How old is your secretary?" Alan asked.

"Twenty-two," Dad said.

"So what do you expect? To her home before midnight *is* only a little late," Alan explained.

"Who are you—the bearded translator of generations?" Dad asked. "The college guru returns?" Dad cleared his throat, then twirled his new mustache.

"Chill out, Dad," Alan said. "There's nothing to get excited about. Hair is a statement."

"Of what?" Grandpa said. "Hair today, gone tomorrow?"

"That's deep, Grandpa," Alan said. "Let me think about that."

The telephone rang. I answered it and handed the receiver to Gary, who was standing behind me. Mom started to laugh again and wipe tears from her eyes. All attention was on her and she didn't even notice Gary, who shrugged his shoulders at me, indicating no news yet about Frieda Weiss.

Mom was talking a mile a minute. "It really was like when we were teenagers," she explained, and stopped to kiss Kerry and Alan, realizing she hadn't greeted them yet. "You kids are going to love this."

We all went into the living room following Mom, Gary included. We sat down and waited for her to continue.

"Your mother and I had some talking to do— some things to work out." Dad started the story because Mom was hysterical laughing again. She caught her breath. "We didn't want to upset any of you. And it's so confusing around here already. We needed a place where we could talk, yell, if we needed to."

"Tell the truth," Mom interrupted my dad. "We needed to be alone. In our marriage we've always tried to take care of problems as soon as we notice one starting and not wait for a crisis. We needed a romantic evening together."

"Way to go, Ma," said Alan.

"So I picked Susan up at the courthouse and we went to Coney Island to pick up some hot dogs and french fries at Nathan's. Then we drove out to Plum Beach—off the Belt Parkway."

"To watch the submarine races?" Grandpa said.

"How can you watch submarine races?" Grandma asked. "Even I know submarines are underwater. What are you talking about, Lou? You know sometimes you make no sense at all." Grandma almost socked Grandpa on his sore shoulder. He blocked her in time.

"Right, Pop," Mom said, and winked.

"They were necking, Minnie, smooching, making out, you call it now?" Grandpa explained, then looked of all places at Gary and me. I almost died.

"Tell them what happened next," Mom said to Dad, and convulsed into laughter again.

"Well," Dad said, and started to chuckle to himself at the thought, "suddenly there was a big light shining on us and a big policeman rapping on the window. Your mother and father got into trouble at age forty-seven for illegal parking and necking at Plum Beach. You tell them the rest of the story," he said to Mom, and she continued.

"I asked this burly, tough policeman, who was about our age, if he was married and he was. Then I described our household of kids, parents, baby grandson, all the wonderful people we love having with us, but needed a short time away from. You know what he did?"

"What?" I asked, curling up on the carpet, tucking my feet under me as if I were waiting for the end of a good bedtime story when I was little. I glanced at Gary. I think he'd gotten involved in the story my parents were telling and relaxed, at least for the moment.

"The policeman turned off his light and said, 'Have a good evening. Just remember times have changed since our teen years. It's not safe to park like this. I tell my kids and I'll tell you—ask for some privacy at home.'"

I now definitely knew that I wasn't the only one with problems living in this house. I hadn't realized how much my parents needed privacy. I know I do, but I didn't think anyone else really did. Something about all this made me feel good. In these days, when you hear so much about divorce, my parents are practically arrested for making out—with each other. But I also got even more worried thinking of that policeman's warning about the way things have changed, the dangers of being out alone at night in the city. Was Gary's grandma in serious danger?

"So," Mom summed it up. "We're all going to have to sit down and work out some plans. I know, Wendy, you've been feeling you're the one whose life has been most affected by all these changes. You should call a family conference, so things can be talked out."

"Change is good to get used to," Grandma said, sounding very wise. "Change is the one thing that stays the same in life—something's always changing," she added in her own kind of logic.

"That's deep, Grandma," Alan interrupted. "I'll have to think about that."

I glanced at Gary sitting next to me on the floor. He was starting to move around restlessly, stretching his legs out, tapping his fingers nervously. This was not the time for me to lead a family conference. Our problems seemed minor compared to Gary's family's.

Just then, I guess maybe Mom must have realized she'd blurted out all this personal stuff and there was a non–family member in the room, because she said to Gary, "We're not usually like this."

133.

"A zoo," Grandpa said. "This place is an absolute zoo."

We filled Mom and Dad in on the crisis with Gary's grandmother. They apologized for taking over the attention and offered to help.

"All we can do is wait and think of other places to look," Gary said. "We can watch the news and see if her photo is shown. It should be on in a couple of minutes."

"I'm so sorry," Mom consoled him. "You must be so worried."

We were gathering around the TV set waiting for the news, when Marissa said, "Doesn't anyone want to know what Mac thinks about Mrs. Weiss's condition?"

"Oh, Marissa, I'm sorry," I said. "I forgot. We really want to hear about it." Gary and I got up and stood behind her. I even put my hands on her shoulders and she didn't shrug them off.

"Mac has two ideas," Marissa explained, then softly added, "I'm afraid one is very sad. But the other is very hopeful."

Gary and I looked at each other and I took his hand and squeezed it.

"This data is correlated for the ages of seventy to seventy-five," Marissa went on. "Mac printed out the symptoms of forgetting recent things but remembering years past in detail, mixing up words, withdrawing, sleeplessness, repeating the same questions, less energy, slowness to learn new things, and preferring familiar faces and places. These symptoms can either be the early stages of a sad, serious disease called Alzheimer's disease, or—and this is the hopeful part—" she paused, "they could also be signals of depression, stress, or overmedication for other ailments. And those things can be helped. Your grandmother's taking a lot of medications that different doctors prescribed for different illnesses. Sometimes medications work against each other."

"Well, if we don't find her soon," Gary said, "she'll be off all the medications—even the ones she must take to stay alive, her heart medication and her blood pressure medication." Gary got more upset as he talked. "If only I didn't take that garbage out. I'm always forgetting it. Why couldn't I have forgotten it tonight?" He clenched his hands into fists.

"The news is going on," Kerry said, and we all gathered around the TV. The news seemed endless, with all kinds of terrible things going on, like shootings, and nuclear plant malfunctions they said were minor. Then, sure enough, a picture of Frieda Weiss was shown. The newscaster gave a phone number to call if anyone had "information as to the whereabouts of this missing woman, who is unable to recognize her location and who is in dire need of medication."

We were all very quiet.

"It will all work out," Grandpa said, and patted Gary on the shoulder. "You'll see. A woman with talking eyes like that."

"What about muggers, or worse?" Gary said.

"I'll never understand why people hurt each other," I said. "It would be so wonderful to live in a safe world where people care about each other." For a moment, when I thought that, a picture of this very household came to mind.

"The world is a good place," Grandma said. "Don't ever forget that. There are more good people than bad."

"You've been out there counting them?" Grandpa interrupted.

Grandma waved her hand in a gesture that said, "Don't pay any attention to him," and went on. "You have to be careful, but you can't walk around scared of everything. You do what you can to make the world better, and you start by being good people yourselves."

"You're okay, Grandma," I said.

Grandma hugged me, then hugged Gary too. He really needed that hug, but I'd felt too shy to give it to him.

I didn't know the adopt-a-dog TV spot was on this late at night, but there it was. I made sure everyone saw the old one-eyed dog and I stared at it dreamily, but now was not the time to say anything more. We were all too concerned about Gary's grandmother.

Steve drove Gary home. "I'll call you tomorrow," Gary said to me. "Thanks, you guys," he added to all of us, "for everything."

I wondered if Gary would have called if all this hadn't happened.

I was moving the beds around to make room for Kerry's sleeping bag when I touched a spiderweb. Automatically I called out, "Daddy—could you help me?"

136.

"What's the matter?" my father asked from the other room.

"A spiderweb," I called back.

"A spiderweb or a spider?" Dad asked, walking into my room.

"A spiderweb," I answered.

"That's nothing to worry about," Mom added as she walked down the hall past my room on the way to hers.

"Well, if there's a web, there must be a spider," I answered. "Something had to make the web. Who made it? It wasn't me!" I could feel myself getting annoyed. Maybe it was just the kind of day it had been. I'd just about had it with everything.

My dad gave a really quick look around the room. "There's no spider," he answered, kissed me goodnight, and went to his room.

Kerry came in, laid out her sleeping bag, and went to stand on line to reserve a turn to take a shower. Seeing her reminded me about what she'd said about independence. How she'd had to learn to handle situations by herself, even when it came to spiders. I decided to give myself Independence Lesson #3. From the box where I keep yarn scraps I got some of the black wool I use to make picture frames. I wound a piece around a button and tied on some strands to look like legs. Then, tossing my homemade spider onto the floor, I stomped it. I picked it up and tossed and stomped again and again. The heels of my shoes made a clicking noise each time I stomped.

Grandpa was walking by my room. He looked in.

"What are you—a Flamingo dancer?" he asked. For a minute I didn't know what he was talking about. Then I had to laugh as he imitated the way I clicked my heels. "I'd clap my hands high over my head if my shoulder wasn't busted," he added.

"A flamenco dancer?" I said. "Is that what you meant?"

"That's what I said," he replied. I'd have to add the mixed-up word to my collection. I couldn't wait to tell Gary and make him laugh.

"You're a good dancer, Grandpa. I didn't know you could dance like they do in Spain."

"Not many people know," he said. "I can tango and hustle, too. I take lessons." He started to sing and do a few steps. He wasn't even embarrassed to dance and sing in front of me. I always needed privacy to do that.

A mixed wave of joy and sadness rolled over me as I thought of how great my grandparents are. It's as if they show the good parts of growing old, and Gary's missing grandmother is the sad side.

A loud shushing sound wound its way down the hall and stopped.

"Who shushed?" Grandpa called. There was no answer. "If someone shushes, they should tell you why," he announced, kissed me good-night, and went off to bed.

Grandma came in just as I stomped the handmade spider a final stomp.

"What a day," she muttered. "Now what are you doing?"

"I'm practicing to be independent," I said. "I'm

practicing to stomp a spider with my own two feet."

"Independence has got nothing to do with spiders," she said. "Take it from me. It has to do with knowing when to ask for people's help, when to do things by yourself, and when it's your turn to do the helping. And when you get older like me, you even think about when it's time to give it up maybe, and consider a senior-citizen or nursing home. I wouldn't ever want to be a burden and wander off and cause worry."

I found myself quoting Alan. "I'll think about that." Only I meant it. Then I added, "You'll never be a burden. Don't talk that way." Grandma took me in her arms and hugged me against her big bosoms.

"We have to find and help that Frieda Weiss," she said. Grandma and I held each other tightly, as if it was a promise we were making to each other. And I have to help that poor old one-eyed dog, I added a silent promise to myself.

14.

THE NEXT MORNING I woke up to the sound of Grandma scolding Mom. "Susan, cook the cereal on a low flame. You're scorching the pot." At breakfast, which had to be served in the dining room because there were so many of us, Grandma gave Grandpa a bowl of steaming hot oatmeal.

"It will soothe your stomach," she said. "So you can stop rubbing your belly and feeling uncomfortable."

"You really should eat bran," Marissa advised from where she was feeding Jory. "What you need is not soothing, but more fiber."

"I like soothing better," Grandpa said, "and I hate bran. If I need more fiber, I'll eat a towel."

I thought that was the funniest line. I wish I could be as funny and quick as Grandpa. Alan, Steve, Kerry, Mom, Dad, and I were laughing. Grandma started to chuckle and, best of all, Marissa finally sat down and laughed, too. I didn't remember breakfasts being funny before Grandma and Grandpa came to stay.

For a while we were so busy enjoying our family that we forgot about the missing Frieda Weiss. Maybe we all figured she'd been found and returned by now.

Earlier Grandma had been running the kitchen as if

it were a restaurant. She took orders, she gave orders, and she was the plate inspector. Those of us who'd had sunny-side-up eggs were being checked. "You're not eating the yolk?" she asked me. "You're wasting it?"

"I can't eat it," I said. "It looks alive."

"People are starving in Africa and you're wasting good egg yolks?" Grandma asked.

"You're really up on the news, Gram," Alan said.

"What do you want her to do. Mail egg yolks to Africa?" Marissa asked. "I mail donations to the Save The Children fund each month. They need money for food more than Wendy's egg yolk." Grandpa laughed first. The rest of us were stunned for a moment. Marissa had actually cracked a joke. Okay, so maybe it was on a subject that is no laughing matter. But it was a try.

"That's good, Marissa," I said. "Very funny." And then we all laughed. Marissa looked pleased.

The phone rang. It was Gary. But he didn't have any news. There'd been no word yet about his grandmother, and he and his parents were very scared and worried. "Come over in forty-five minutes. I should finally get my turn in the shower soon and be dressed by then," I told him. "We'll go out and search for your Grandma some more. We'll find her. You'll see." I offered my help and comfort. I wished I could do more. He didn't sound comforted and he wasn't joking at all. He sounded awful. I hung up and headed for the bathroom.

Sometimes when I'm in the shower and the hot water (if there is any left) is pouring onto me, and my head is all soapy with shampoo, I feel like no time is passing and I get good ideas. Now, as I washed my hair, I thought about independence, which reminded me of last night's conversation with Grandma. Then I pictured Frieda Weiss and some ideas connected.

I got dressed as quickly as I could. Kerry could see I was uptight, and even offered to paint a flower on my fingernail like the kids do at college. I told her maybe later.

Grandma, Grandpa, Mom, Dad, and Alan went to Saturday morning services at synagogue. "I'll ask God personally to look for Frieda Weiss," Grandma told me, "and I'll also explain that you and Gary are doing the legwork and searching for her, too."

Before they left, Marissa asked to talk to Mom and Dad privately. I'm very curious about what that was about.

I was standing in the foyer waiting for Gary. The phone was nearby and while I waited, I couldn't resist the urge to call the telephone number I've seen so many times on the adopt-a-dog commercial. I just had to find out if the old one-eyed dog had been adopted yet.

"Hello," I said, "my name is Wendy Meyer and I'm calling to find out if that one-eyed dog on the TV spot last night has been adopted yet. I'm not calling to adopt it. I wish I could. I just wanted to know about it."

"Thank you for calling, Ms. Meyer. We've run the ad for that dog several times over the past year and a half. We keep trying. It's a wonderful dog but one that is always left over—very difficult to place. Besides its having only one eye, no one wants a dog that might only live another five years."

"Oh no?" I said, then added, "I have to go now.

Thanks, and please tell the leftover dog hello from Wendy, and to hang in there. Okay?"

"Sure." The woman laughed and hung up.

Gary arrived. He had dark circles under his eyes, like he hadn't slept at all. "I've got an idea of a possible place your Grandma might be," I said, but I didn't tell him that it came to me in the shower. I put on my jacket, and shouted, "I'm going."

"Where are we going?" Gary said, walking fast to keep up with me as I headed out the door, down the street, and up Avenue K.

"To Coney Island Avenue—to the nursing home," I announced, thinking no one would have thought of that.

"Thanks anyway, Wendy," Gary said. "My parents called nursing homes all over the city last night to see if anyone had picked Grandma up and brought here there. No luck."

I stopped walking. I'd had such a strong picture in my mind when I was in that shower of Frieda Weiss sitting in the visitors' room at the nursing home and me finding her, being the heroine, and having Gary love me for it.

I don't really believe in supernatural stuff, but on *Donahue* last summer I saw this woman who even the police hire to find missing children. She said everyone has parts of their brain they've never used and that her powers weren't supernatural. Maybe in the shower I'd used a new piece of brain. Who's to say? I usually can't even find Jennifer and Brenda in a movie theater unless they yell to me.

143.

"Let's go over there anyway," I said. "Sometimes you just have to listen to a hunch. We have to visit and talk to a couple of older people as the last part of the health project anyway. Maybe some of my friends there might have ideas as to where they would go if they were your grandmother."

"Now that's a good idea. It can't hurt anyway," Gary said, and we picked up our pace. A police car passed by from the 73rd Precinct, and I wondered if the officer was looking for Mrs. Weiss.

There are some benches outside the nursing home, and it was a sunny day, kind of warm for November. I said hello to the elderly man and woman sitting there, then we went inside.

The nurse at the station recognized me and said that Mr. Mason and Mrs. Rabinowitz still talk about the picture frames I made for them. That made me feel good. I asked her if I could speak to them.

"Sure," she said, "we welcome all visitors here. We even just started a peer counseling program to encourage older people to come in and visit, to help the folks here keep in touch with the world. We've got a day-care program, too, and you may be interested in helping out with our newest project: 'Hug-a-pet.' We've found our people here really perk up if they can pet a dog or kitten."

"I don't have any pets," I said sadly. Then I changed the subject back to Mrs. Weiss. "Would you know if someone was brought here during the night?" I asked. Gary explained about his grandmother's disappearance and showed her the photo. His parents had only given a description over the phone.

The nurse checked the records. "No," she said. "We've had no new admissions. The photo looks just a bit familiar, but we've had a lot of older folks in and out over the past week, training sessions for that peer counseling program I was telling you about. No one's been brought in. That I'd know. Sorry."

We thanked her and went to find my friends, Mrs. Rabinowitz and Mr. Mason. This place smells more like a hotel than like a hospital, I thought as I walked down the shiny, clean hall with rails along the wall. I looked in every room we passed. But there was no Mrs. Weiss. Again, I thought of what Grandma had said to me last night, about how at her age she sometimes thinks about when it might be time to give up her independence and consider a nursing home or senior-citizen apartment. She'd had a tear in her eye but a very stubborn, strong voice when she'd said, "I wouldn't ever want to be a burden."

"Is your grandmother a stubborn type?" I asked Gary as we stopped to look around the visitors' room.

"She always was," he said. "She once had 'pressure in her chest,' she'd called it, 'and dizziness,' and wouldn't call a doctor to see if it was a heart attack because it was the weekend and she said, 'He needs to be with his family and it's only gas.' She made me promise not to tell my parents because my dad and mom were going out to dinner with Dad's boss, and she didn't want to spoil their evening."

"That's stubborn all right." I laughed. "So she would never want to be a burden, either." Gary didn't quite understand what I meant. I had this feeling I was onto something. That I had all the pieces but they were scattered around and didn't make sense yet. Gary was looking very serious and sad, so I switched to a Charlie Chan accent and pretended to twirl a mustache. "If deductions correct, number one son will find Grandmother hiding in room here," I said.

"You like old Charlie Chan movies too?" Gary said, and his eyes brightened a bit.

I explained what Grandma had said to me, and my theory.

Number one: His grandmother didn't want to be a burden and went off.

Number two: Maybe, if Marissa's information, the hopeful part, about Mrs. Weiss perhaps taking too much medication and her dosage needing regulating, was true, she could think a bit clearer when the over-medication wore off.

Number three: She'd lived in the neighborhood all her life and, according to Kerry's information after phoning the telephone numbers in Mrs. Weiss's address book, had a few friends right in this nursing home.

Number four: The nurse here said there were older people coming in and out all week for training sessions on peer counseling. Mrs. Weiss would have fit right in.

Number five: I had a strong hunch she was here.

I felt very good figuring all this out. I'm used to using my imagination for singing and dancing, making things, and dreaming about traveling. Now I felt the same good feeling as I used my imagination to figure out where Frieda Weiss might be.

"Call Kerry and see if she remembers the names of

the friends of my grandma who now live here," Gary suggested. "That'll save time."

"Good idea," I said, and we went to the phone booth at the end of the hall. I called and Kerry gave us the names we needed. We told my friend, the head nurse, my theory and the names, and she looked at this list of the names of residents and told us their room numbers. We headed for a Mrs. Dennis's room.

"A woman by that name used to be a waitress at Grandma and Grandpa's restaurant," Gary explained. "She always pinched my cheeks when I was little."

We found the room and knocked on the door. "Come in," a voice called, and we opened the door and stepped inside. Mrs. Frankle, whose name was also on the list, was there too. Gary thought he remembered them and said who he was. I noticed they both looked at the closed bathroom door.

Mrs. Dennis pinched Gary's cheeks and squealed, "You're all grown up."

Our eyes exchanged a glance of understood silent giggles. Then the bathroom door opened and a very surprised Frieda Weiss walked out.

This was turning into a terrific day. Mrs. Weiss hugged Gary and patted his head. "What are you doing here?" he asked softly. "We love you, Grandma. We were very worried. Do you understand what I'm saying?" He spoke very slowly.

Mrs. Weiss sank down into the armchair by the window and sighed. She sounded weak as she spoke. "Right now I understand more than I have understood for a long time," she said feebly. "My head isn't buzz-

147.

ing. The world doesn't look like a double exposure on a photograph. It's easier to understand that way."

"But what about your heart medicine. You can't miss more than two times—the doctor said." Gary did the talking now. I just leaned back, feeling like I'd been in a scene on *General* when things are worked out.

"I didn't miss two times. Mrs. Dennis gave me one of hers. I saw she was going to take the same pill I take and I asked her for it. But I didn't take anything else," Mrs. Weiss explained.

"You gave her your medicine?" Gary asked Mrs. Dennis.

"What are friends for?" she answered. "I could skip one time. Nothing happens. Anyway—for thirty years I've taken orders from your grandmother. One more order felt good."

"But Grandma, don't you know it's dangerous to take someone else's medicine?" Gary said.

"Believe me, it was more dangerous for me not to take that heart pill. I've been taking those pills for years. I know what they look like. And I think some of them make me feel sick. Who are you?" Gary's grandmother noticed me standing by the doorway and changed the subject.

"Grandma, this is my girlfriend Wendy," Gary introduced me, and I almost flipped. I have never in my entire life been a boy's girlfriend. Mrs. Dennis and Mrs. Frankle winked.

"I think I've seen your girlfriend while I was visiting here. She's a nice one, but I thought *I* was your best girl," Mrs. Weiss teased Gary. "I'm away one day and it's over?"

"You'll always be my best girl." Gary wasn't even shy about walking over and kissing her. "You're not a burden, you know. I know you heard me fight with Mom and Dad about staying with you, but I didn't mean to make you feel like a burden."

"I know, sweety," Mrs. Weiss said. "I wasn't thinking. I don't remember too much about last night. I think I probably wandered around in circles for a while, then I guess I must have started to go to where the restaurant used to be. When my head cleared a little, I saw I wasn't even near the restaurant, but sitting on the bench outside this place, and I remembered visiting Mrs. Dennis and Mrs. Frankle here. I needed a friend so much."

Mrs. Dennis reached over and patted Gary's grandmother's hand.

"People were coming in and out, so I went in and found an empty room to sleep in for the night. I was so exhausted. Then, this morning, when the coast was clear, I found Mrs. Dennis and Mrs. Frankle. They fed me their food and helped me to see how I must be worrying my family. I was just going to call home."

"We *were* worried," Gary interrupted.

"Last night I didn't even think about worrying anyone, to tell you the truth," Mrs. Weiss said. "But I'm ready to go home now."

Gary called his dad and he came and picked us up. Gary looks a lot like him. Mr. Weiss was very grateful

149.

and thanked me about ten times for my help in finding his mother. The nurse at the desk told him and Gary's grandmother more about the new day-care program and the peer counseling.

It was quite a day. It felt really good to help someone. But the next day it also sure felt good when I found out that someone had helped me.

That evening was filled with "Tales of Mrs. Weiss." We didn't get to have our family conference, to work out some plans for meeting everyone's needs, till Sunday at dinner. Family conferences, as a way to solve problems, have been a tradition in the Meyer household for as long as I can remember. Whoever has the problem calls the conference and leads it, so everyone, in turn, gets a chance to speak up. This usually works okay when it's just Mom, Dad, my brothers and sister, and me, but tonight when I called the conference this wasn't easy because there were so many more of us and everyone was talking at once. Jory started to cry and Kerry had to pack up her sweaters and get ready to go back to college. She and Alan were being picked up by friends. Alan had already packed up his freshly laundered belongings and was ready.

"Who are you, baa baa black sheep with your three laundry bags full?" Grandpa joked.

It took me a while to get some order. Then Alan spoke. He had not shaved off his beard or gotten his hair cut, and *his* need to express himself, along with Dad's same need, was made clear to all. Grandma spoke up and so did Marissa. She got Grandma to agree to read the Dr. Pepper Feinback book if Marissa agreed to let Grandma explain her disagreements, should she have them.

Marissa told me she wanted us to get along better. I hadn't realized her life had been changed so much, too. She's an only child, used to her own ways. She'd always done lots of things very well. Moving in here made her feel she had to prove she was still independent. I guess she must have found this household overwhelming, just as I did. It seemed we had more in common than I'd thought. Mom's circus act of juggling everybody's needs was put to rest as we all worked things out together. Mom, Dad, Marissa, and Steve brought up the issue of privacy. That was a big part of my problem, too.

I must admit I came up with a most terrific plan for privacy for all, at least for the next few months while Grandpa and Grandma stay with us. It dawned on me that only a few miles away sits Grandpa's empty studio apartment. The details of which days or weekends Marissa and Steve get to use it, and which days Mom and Dad get to use it, are still to be worked out. I get to fix up my own private, "do not enter space" in our basement. What was funny was that when I said I need a place to sing and dance, Mom and Dad were surprised. "We didn't even know you like to do those things," Mom said.

"I think that's great fun," Dad added.

And Marissa quietly said, "I like to do jazzercise."

"Maybe I'll do jazzercise with you sometimes," I said, and I even smiled at her for an instant. I didn't want to send either of us into a state of shock, so

151.

this was not an invitation to become best friends or anything.

Kerry spoke up and invited me to spend a weekend away at her college sometime. That would be a good independence lesson.

Then I got to my most important need. Need of a very special, one-eyed, old dog. "I've found the perfect adopt-a-dog," I announced. "It's big enough to protect me from intruders and gentle enough so it won't bother Jory. It's housebroken, and old enough so it won't be a responsibility in five years when I go off to college."

"What's one more in a zoo like this?" Grandpa said.

"And a dog doesn't even use the shower!" I added.

Mom and Dad laughed. "I think you've covered everything," Dad said. Then Mom explained that this morning Marissa had told them all about how much I needed that dog—something I could take care of and make decisions about. She'd said, there's a book on teenagers by Dr. Haim Ginott that recommends giving teenagers responsibility. Marissa even offered to take care of the dog in years to come when she, Steve, and Jory will be on their own.

"Marissa is not the enemy." Mom whispered that part to me.

"I don't exactly love having her here, but I'll give her a chance," I whispered back. "So do I get the dog?" I asked.

"Marissa made all the arrangements. We pick the one-eyed dog up tomorrow," Dad said.

I didn't care who saw me. I was so happy I went into

152.

my *Chorus Line* number with everyone watching! They even applauded. "Thanks, Marissa," I added, whirling over to her and ending with a hug. A kiss I'd have to work up to but the hug was sincere.

A while later, when Kerry and Alan left, this very same house seemed bigger. It was really odd.

I spent the evening making phone calls to tell Jennifer and Brenda about this crazy weekend and to tell Gary, my boyfriend, that I was getting to adopt a dog—tomorrow.

Epilogue

THE DAYS HAVE been going so fast. It's Thanksgiving today. Kerry and Alan came in to fill up on turkey. Alan brought a girlfriend home. She's nice and very bright. Dad says maybe she'll straighten him out. The whole house smells like garlic and butter. Grandma, Marissa, and Mom are cooking three turkeys, and my dog Spot and I are walking around sniffing the air and drooling. I feel as if I could eat an entire turkey myself. Thanksgiving is my favorite holiday. It smells so good and the next day everyone loves leftovers.

Mom and Dad let me invite Gary, his parents, and grandmother to join us. Grandma said if she plans to open a restaurant she better practice cooking in quantity.

Mrs. Weiss is having a lot of medical tests at the hospital where Steve is so the doctors can find the right combinations of medication for her. All the tests aren't back yet, but Steve said, from what he could tell, he didn't think she had Alzheimer's disease. Mrs. Weiss enrolled herself in the day-care program at the nursing home and Grandpa is thinking of becoming a peer volunteer there. He went with me when I took Spot for the hug-a-pet program.

Mr. Mason, Mrs. Rabinowitz, Mrs. Dennis, and Mrs. Frankle love it when I bring Spot. Grandpa summed it up: "An old dog like that understands what an ache is."

We're becoming more flexible, Marissa and me. We do jazzercise together to stretch our muscles, computer games to stretch our minds, and we try to give each other plenty of space and privacy to stretch our independence. We still fight though, particularly about Dr. Pepper Feinback's advice about babies and about watching *General Hospital*, but the time between fights is stretching. Sometimes I even get so involved working on the computer, I miss a crisis moment on *General*.

I had so many detention makeups over the last two weeks that I had plenty of time to work on my health project about the life cycle. I was really glad that Mrs. Devin gave us most of our papers back yesterday, and superglad that she has a sense of humor. Gary and I both got A's on babies and mid-life. We didn't get old age back yet except for the summary part. The three different characters and lifestyles of the elderly that I wrote about were: one, Grandma wanting to start a restaurant business; two, Grandpa and the temporary problems of health; three, Mrs. Dennis—life at a nursing home.

Gary and I have been an item in school for two weeks now. We hold hands in assembly and lunch. Robby did call Brenda again, but they're not a pair. She and Jennifer have been pretty understanding about how much time I spend with Gary, and I make sure I walk home with them.

Gary and his parents should be here any minute now. "Wendy!" My father called. "Do you know where my distance glasses are?"

"Far away," I answered, and laughed at my own joke.

The Macy's Thanksgiving Day Parade was on TV, and Spot, Jory, and I went in to watch it. An adopt-a-dog commercial went on. A picture showed the one-eyed, older dog with the word ADOPTED across it. "See, Spot," I said, and while holding Jory carefully with one hand, I sat down on the carpet next to Spot. I directed his eye to the screen and kissed him on his nose. "Look, you're on TV. You're famous!"

Sometimes I worry about how I'll feel when everyone starts to leave my house and I'm alone again. There should be a health course on worrying. They never teach you about that. I've decided that independence has something to do with not needing it so much. I don't know if that makes sense but I know what I mean. I want to be on my own but know that my family is there for me and I'm there for them. Maybe that *is* independence. Anyway, I figure being a leftover kid again will be Lesson #1 of my new plan to get used to changes and . . . I'll still have my dog Spot.

Health Project

Part II: Teenage and Mid-Life

List five of your concerns as teenagers:
1. Independence and freedom.

2. Popularity.
3. Will I fit in at high school and later at college? And will I be able to find my way around?
4. Will my hair ever look right?
5. What will I look like when I'm finished with braces and retainer?

List five of your parents' concerns in mid-life:

1. Letting go of kids.
2. Finding time alone (independence and freedom).
3. What they look like (trying to look and act young and worrying if their hair looks right, including counting gray hairs or hairs in the sink).
4. Worries about their parents.
5. How to pay for college.

List five things your parents frequently tell you:

1. Watch your mouth.
2. What time will you be home? Who are you going with? Where are you going? Will there be a parent home? And call if you're going to be late.
3. Don't forget your keys.
4. Don't open the doors for strangers or ever go close to a stranger's car.
5. Clean your room. It's a fire hazard. At least clear a path.

Write a composition about something that signifies a parent's entrance into mid-life or mid-life crisis.

sentence too long. Break in two.

Your Father's Mustache
by Wendy Meyer

If your father comes back from a sales conference and walks into the house with his hand covering the upper part of his lip and then kisses you and you feel a scratchiness that you never felt before, your father may have just signaled his entrance into Mid-life or Mid-life crisis. You must now get ready to face . . . Your father's mustache. You must face it at meals including veal parmagan *[sp]* when the mozzarella cheese gets caught in it. You must face it when it is worn along with a jogging outfit. And you must not laugh at your fathers mustache as it quivers while he scolds you for having a big mouth or funnier yet for getting a new kind of mod hair cut and telling you how strange it looks.

you need an apostrophe

Final Summary—Describe the life-cycle in your own way and your feelings about it.

My household! And it's great!

(A) Wendy— your sense of humor will be your strength throughout your entire life cycle. a job well done! Mrs. Devin

158.